THE ACTUAL

Also by Saul Bellow

*It All Adds Up: From the Dim Past to the
Uncertain Future*

Something to Remember Me By

The Bellarosa Connection

A Theft

More Die of Heartbreak

*Him with His Foot in His Mouth
and Other Stories*

The Dean's December

*To Jerusalem and Back: A Personal
Account*

Humboldt's Gift

Mr. Sammler's Planet

Mosby's Memoirs and Other Stories

Herzog

Henderson the Rain King

Seize the Day

The Adventures of Augie March

The Victim

Dangling Man

THE ACTUAL

Saul Bellow

Viking

VIKING
Published by the Penguin Group
Penguin Books USA Inc., 375 Hudson Street,
New York, New York 10014, U.S.A.
Penguin Books Ltd, 27 Wrights Lane,
London W8 5TZ, England
Penguin Books Australia Ltd, Ringwood,
Victoria, Australia
Penguin Books Canada Ltd, 10 Alcorn Avenue,
Toronto, Ontario, Canada M4V 3B2
Penguin Books (N.Z.) Ltd, 182–190 Wairau Road,
Auckland 10, New Zealand

Penguin Books Ltd, Registered Offices:
Harmondsworth, Middlesex, England

First published in 1997 by Viking Penguin,
a division of Penguin Books USA Inc.

1   3   5   7   9   10   8   6   4   2

LIBRARY OF CONGRESS CATALOGING IN PUBLICATION DATA
Bellow, Saul.
The actual : a novella / Saul Bellow.
p.   cm.
ISBN 0–670–86075–1 (alk. paper)
I. Title.
PS3503.E4488A63   1997
813'.52—dc21   96–51173

This book is printed on acid-free paper. ∞

Printed in the United States of America
Set in Weiss
Designed by Jaye Zimet

THE ACTUAL

It's easy enough to see what people *think* they're doing. Nor is what they really are up to hard for common sense to make out. The usual repertories of stratagems, deceits, personality rackets, ringing the changes on criminal cunning, are hardly worth examining. Years have gone by since I last found interest in *The Psychopathology of Everyday Life* and its once fresh story-behind-the-story. That a slip of the tongue will lead you back to the mischievous id needs no more proving. I grant that Freud was one of the most ingenious men who ever lived, but I have no more use for his system than I have for Paley's watch—a metaphor for the universe, wound up in the beginning, then ticking away for billions of years. As long as a single thing is there to suppose, somebody (in this case an eighteenth-century English clergyman) will be sure to suppose it.

To become known was never a special desire with me. And I do not feel that I would be hard for a good observer to make out. When asked, I say that I live in Chicago and am semiretired, but I never care to specify my trade. Not that there is much to hide. But something about me hints that there is. I have a Chinese look. After the Korean War, I was sent to study Chinese in a special school. Maybe my esoteric skills, by a process of secret suggestion, brought an East Asian expression into my face. The kids at school never called me "Chink"—and they might have done it because I was in an ambiguous category, an outsider, an orphan. But that, too, was misleading. Both my parents were alive. I was put in an orphanage because my mother had a disease of the joints that sent her from sanitarium to sanitarium, mainly abroad. My father was a simple carpenter. The bills were paid by my mother's family, her brothers being successful sausage manufacturers and able to afford the cures she took at Bad Nauheim or Hot Springs, Arkansas.

I was assumed at school to be one of the children from the orphanage. I had no occasion to explain my special circumstances, and all the peculiarities of those circumstances sank into the structure of my face—a round head, hair worn as long as the orphanage allowed, a pair of fat black eyes, a wide mouth with a sizable lip. Wonderful materials for the insidious Fu Manchu look.

A man's road back to himself is a return from his spiritual exile, for that is what a personal history amounts to—exile. I didn't allow myself to make too much of the Chinese lip. I seem to have decided that to be busy about one's self-image, to adjust, revise, to tamper with it, was a waste of time.

In the days when I was reviewing my options, I believed that I might—just might—effect a transfer to another civilization. The Chinese would never notice me in China, while in my own country, looking vaguely Chinese would not be enough to prevent discovery . . . I probably mean exposure.

But I lasted only five years in the Far East; the last two of these I spent in Burma, where I made important business connections, discovering while immersed in another civilization that I had something of a gift for putting together business deals. Provided with a lifetime income through the Burmese operation, which had a Guatemalan branch, I returned to Chicago, where my emotional roots were.

I gave up being a Chinaman. Some Westerners of course preferred to be Oriental. There was the famous British hermit of Peking described so beautifully by Trevor-Roper; there was also Two-Gun Cohen, the Montreal gangster hired by Sun Yat-sen to be his bodyguard, and who never wished to return to Canada, it seems.

You will see soon enough that I had substantial reasons for resettling in Chicago. I might have gone elsewhere—to Baltimore or Boston—but the difference between cities is more of the same, superficially disguised. In Chicago I had unfinished emotional business. In Boston or in Baltimore I would still have thought, daily and regularly, of the same woman—of what I might have said to her, of what she might have answered. "Love objects," as psychiatry has named them, are not frequently come by or easily put aside. "Distance" is really a formality. The mind takes no real notice of it.

I returned to Chicago and opened a business on Van Buren Street. I trained my employees to run it for me, and then I was free to fill my life with more interesting activities. Somewhat to my own surprise, I became part of a set of curious people. The main threat in a place like Chicago is emptiness—human gaps and breaks, a sort of spiritual ozone that smells like bleach. In the old days, Chicago streetcars gave off such a smell. Ozone is made by a combination of oxygen and ultraviolet rays in the upper atmosphere.

I found ways to protect myself from this liminal threat (the threat of being sucked into outer space). Oddly enough, I began to be invited out as a man who knew a lot about the Orient. At least, hostesses believed I did—*I* made no claim. One didn't have to say much.

I settled into an apartment on the edge of Lincoln Park. And pretty soon I had a significant piece of luck. I met old Sigmund Adletsky and Mrs. Adletsky at a dinner party. Adletsky is a name instantly recognized everywhere, like Prince Charles or Donald Trump—or, in earlier times, the Shah of Iran or Basil Zaharoff. Yes, Adletsky, the old Chief himself, the founding colossus, the man under whom the incomparable luxury hotel complex on the Caribbean coast of Mexico was built—one of many pleasure domes on the subtropical beaches of many continents. Old Adletsky had by now turned his empire over to his sons and grandchildren. He would never have bothered with the likes of me if he had still been running the hotels, the airlines, the mines, the electronics laboratories.

The dinner party at which we met was given by Frances Jellicoe. A Jellicoe commanded the British Grand Fleet in the Battle of Jutland (1916). The family had an American branch (so the American Jellicoes said), which was very rich. Frances, who came into a fortune, had also inherited a collection of paintings that included a Bosch, a Botticelli, and several Goya portraits, as well as some Picassos of my favorite kind—multiple noses and eyes. I greatly admired (esteemed) Frances. Fritz Rourke, her husband and the father of her two children, had divorced her, but she continued to love him, and not in the abstract. He was there that night, drunk and noisy, and the most conspicuous thing about the man was the quality or grade of the love to be seen in his ex-wife as she stood up for him. A stout woman, she had never been pretty. That night in her Gold Coast dining room, her face was aflame, and the lower lip was drawn away from the teeth. Rourke soon was drunk; he quickly got out of hand, breaking glasses. She took her stand behind the uncontrollable former husband's chair, making a silent statement of despair, militancy, loyalty. Well, to me she was a rich human asset. Not the millions in her trust account, but her character—a character of great price.

Old Adletsky was sitting at my table, and he, too, was taking it all in. My guess is that few things of this nature occurred in the presence of a man so rich. For him, what happened during dinner may have been something like a return to earlier, immigrant days. To be a trillionaire is like living in a controlled environment, I imagine. He was a little guy, shrunken by his great age. Not very big to begin with. In the New World, his immigrant melting-pot generation of malnourished teeny-weenies produced six-foot sons and large, luxuriant daughters. I myself was both larger and heavier than my parents, though internally more fragile, perhaps.

I didn't expect Adletsky to take note of my presence, and I was surprised a few days after the dinner party by a note from the old man's secretary. I was requested to call his office for an appointment. At the bottom of the note were two words in Adletsky's own hand: "Please do." Nearly a century ago, he had been taught to write in Cyrillic or, more probably, Hebrew characters, judging by the scrollwork of the capital *P*.

Thoroughly trained in the Adletsky system, the appointments secretary was unable to tell me, on the phone, why I was asked to come in. So I visited him in his glassy lair, his penthouse office suite. I went downtown and was conducted to an express elevator, activated by a special key. I felt about this swift ride as I used to feel about the pneumatic tubes that once connected department store salespersons to the cashiers. The sales slips and the dollar bills were sucked into the pipe, and—*snick-snick*—here are the new socks and there is your change.

You no longer face an executive across his desk. You sit with him on a divan. Beside you is a coffee table with a demitasse, a dish of sugar cubes.

I sensed that I was thickening my face defensively under Adletsky's scrutiny. The old man had no need to ask personal questions. My life and deeds had been sifted by members of his staff. Evidently I had survived the preliminary screening. He had been so fully briefed that there would be no talk about my origins, education, accomplishments— thank God.

He said, "At Frances Jellicoe's dinner, the name Jim Thorpe came up, and only you could identify the college that wonderful athlete came from. . . ."

"Carlisle," I said. "In Pennsylvania. An Indian school."

"You have no special interest in this; you just happened to know it. Do you have lots of general information in your head? Excuse me for asking, Mr. Trellman, but when was the Federal Reserve Bank established?"

"Back in 1913? . . . 'Harry' is good enough."

I could see that he was pleased, though in the penthouse dazzle I felt that all my "preparations" were disintegrating. Preparations? Well, the title of Stanislavsky's famous book is *An Actor Prepares*. Everybody prepares, and ascribes to others a power to judge, grants them the possession of standards that may be nonexistent.

I moved toward the shady side of the settee.

What Adletsky had gotten from me so far was random information of the sort useful in solving crossword puzzles. Of course, all this was preliminary. He behaved like a technician inspecting the model of an advanced device. What would a doctor have said about so small and old and wrinkled a creature as Adletsky? And so rich. Superrich. Rich beyond the comprehension of most people. My comprehension too. With so much dough, I was thinking, you bypassed democracy. You signaled that you were grateful for the opportunities democratic capitalist America had given you; meantime, in your inmost mind, you have streaked away on your own, you have grasped yourself as a pharaoh, the representative of the sun.

"I wanted to talk about Frances Jellicoe," he said.

"Excuse me?"

"Her dinner party. I've always liked Frances. Are you there often?"

"No. She bought some Chinese pieces from me . . ."

"You deal in that stuff."

"Antiquities . . ."

"Why, sure. You import them in damaged condition from China and you fix 'em up in Guatemala City with cheap labor."

"You've researched me," I said. Not that it mattered; my operation, my racket, was sufficiently legal.

"No harm in it," said Adletsky. "I saw you looking on, at Frances."

"A bad moment that was," I said.

"Yes, the husband—the ex—is a loser, an obvious no-good. Frances's mother was what the *Tribune* in the old days called 'a social leader.' The Potter Palmers, the McCormicks, and other micks whose husbands were chairmen of boards and whose daughters had 'coming-out' parties—Frances was one of those."

"Yes, I've met ladies who knew her at finishing school. She *was* a slim gentle creature, once. . . ."

He looked curiously at me when I said "gentle

creature," as if surprised that a man who looked like me should put things in such a way. "But you mean now she's built like a brick shithouse," Adletsky said.

"And then again, her health is very bad—she's fragile, her life is in danger. She has that terrible cortisone swelling, and it makes her look like Babe Ruth."

"Of course; that's the right description," said Adletsky.

"You don't need me, Mr. Adletsky," I said. "Not with the intelligence-gathering service that told you everything there is to know about the Guatemala side of my operation."

"Yes," he said. "But you don't have such a research facility. You have to think, you have to notice and put facts together for yourself. Now that Rourke, the ex-husband, has done himself in the eye. Here is an executive—he made a student from Greenland pregnant, an Eskimo girl. And she sued. Right? That's an item. It's been in the papers."

"Frances and Rourke were divorced years ago. But he remained on the board of various corporations."

"Go on," Adletsky said. "We both think highly of her. And we can't hurt Frances by laying out the data."

"Her father was an Insull partner," I said. "And her grandfather a founder of Commonwealth Edison. She got Rourke made a paid corporate officer in half a dozen other companies."

"Freeloader. Part of the freight many a company carries."

"They got rid of him when the Eskimo girl said she was having his baby," I said. "The purpose of the dinner party was to rehabilitate Rourke socially."

"For the sake of his children?"

"Up to a point," I said. "Also to do her will. To have her way."

"She's not long for this world," said Adletsky. "And she married for love."

"There's the powerful female system we call Frances, and its basic investment is in this lout."

"Nothing else can explain what happened the other night. Would you kindly lay the event out as you saw it."

"All right," I said, more willing than I usually am to speak my mind. As a rule, I am reluctant to put myself on record. I've never operated that way—frankly, directly. I felt, however, that old Adletsky had opened a door for me, for reasons I couldn't readily understand, and that it would be unwise to refuse to come in. Not injurious but, in some way, unsociable. "She invited leaders of the business establishment. I was sitting next to old Ike Cressy of the Continental Bank. You were there for the same general purpose."

"We'd never touch the likes of that husband of hers."

"That's for you only to say, but you were there to increase the gravity of the occasion."

"And you?"

"I was representing the arts. She owns world-famous paintings. There was one guy from Sears, Roebuck. Also one federal judge and What's-his-name from the commodities exchange. And the wives, of course."

And Rourke, drinking and acting up. He was rough and angry—aggressive. He went through a couple of bottles of wine and made a speech denouncing wetbacks and Asian immigrants. He said there were too many unacceptable people already in the country. Then, with a sweep of the arms, he overturned the wineglasses on his side of the table, cracking some of them. I had to remember that Frances's little white Scottie was only half house-broken. On an earlier visit, I had seen him raise his leg to the skirts of armchairs and sofas.

"About Cressy: he started a conversation about Shakespeare at his end of the table. He said the secondary schools had gone to hell, and one reason was that poetry was no longer memorized by the kids. He gave an example of the New York businessman who was kidnapped. Two of this man's employees dug a hole—well, a grave. They snatched and held him in it under a piece of sheet iron. The guy of course thought this was it—he'd never again see the light of day."

"A real piece of major viciousness," said Adletsky. "Do you think the people committing such a crime have any idea what it was—a living grave?"

"They may not have the capacity. But what Cressy said was that the poetry the elderly businessman had learned at school kept him alive."

Bankers do like to quote from Hamlet:

Neither a borrower nor a lender be;
For loan oft loses both itself and friend,
And borrowing dulls the edge of husbandry.

I didn't discuss this with old Adletsky. He would have had no use for such asides. What he wanted was my comment on what happened when Frances picked up her camera from the sideboard.

"You were watching. You saw. She lined all the guests up for a photo," Adletsky said.

"Cressy wasn't going to have his picture taken. Not with Rourke," I said.

"So you picked up on that," said Adletsky.

He was pleased with me. "Who, besides you and me, saw that a battle was developing, Cressy turning his head aside just as she was pressing the camera button? And three times she got the back of his head."

"It was the sole, the only purpose of her dinner. She came up to Cressy and took him by the wrist—forced him to look her in the face."

"There aren't too many observant people

around, are there?" said Adletsky. "Although every-body knew about Rourke and the girl studying to be a midwife. It was in the *Sun-Times*. Frances was furious about the coverage. She despises types like Cressy. I thought she was going to deck him. She's almost big enough. Well, he isn't much, is he?" Adletsky went on. "He's got a condom over his heart. There's nothing human about bank officers."

"That's it," I said, "her one and only motive was to rehabilitate her children's father."

"No. She loves that clumsy Rourke prick. Any worthwhile man would be proud to tap into the loy-alty of a fine broad like Frances. And it had to be Cressy, with Rourke, smiling into the camera. What social credentials have *I* got, an old Jew—or even the guy from Sears? I could make a better man than him out of a piece of wood. . . . What kind of name is Cressy?"

"Could be from Crécy, a French battlefield."

Adletsky had no use for informational sidebars.

"She didn't get her way, poor girl," he said.

All signs were that Frances was headed down-ward. The food was inferior; the table linen was not up to standards, nor was the "staff"; the doggy was wetting the skirts of the sofas. Her color when Cressy enraged her was a murky sort of rust.

"I kept an eye on you as you watched that scene," said Adletsky. "I haven't had much time for social life or psychology items. But now I'm out of planning, acquisitions—I'm out of business action. I go around with my wife on *her* circuit. Anyway, I thought I'd like to become acquainted with somebody like you—a first-class noticer, obviously."

There was nothing I could say to this. Should I tell him that I was sorry his active life had ended—that he was in humanly reduced circumstances?

"I like the way you put things together," Adletsky resumed. "In my business life, I tried to imitate Franklin D. Roosevelt in one respect. I saw that it was a good idea to have a brain trust. Back in '33, he gathered his professors around him. The country had to innovate, or it would go down. . . ."

His English had advanced together with his perspectives as a promoter on a planetary scale. He and his corporate-trained sons and Yale Law School daughters had moved up and up from sphere to sphere, no limit to their adaptability.

"So you had a Roosevelt-style brain trust?"

"No. I had people it benefited me to consult, and I'd like to arrange occasional meetings with you, to be filled in on this or that. I wouldn't have believed that of all the people present, only you and I understood the clinch Frances got into with Cressy."

He was right. Few people can take such things in.

"I'm not all that good at business," I said.

"For business I don't need you. Don't even try to

advise me. I'll only now and then ask you. In my active years I did very little socializing. I have to do it now. And there must be a way to make it pleasanter."

I said, with my usual reserve, that I'd be very pleased to be a part of his brain trust.

"You can satisfy your curiosity about me, too, up to a point," he said. "Of course, you'll have to be discreet. But I think you already are keeping thousands and thousands of things to yourself. You have that look. Has anybody ever told you what a Japanese face you have?"

"Chinese, I always thought."

"Japanese," he insisted.

When I got home, I undressed and examined myself in the long bathroom mirror. The old man was right, you know. I have Japanese legs, straight from one of Hokusai's bath scenes. The thighs are muscular, and the shins are concave. I'd look even more Japanese if I were to shorten my hair and wear a fringe. I began to revise my image accordingly.

For years, since, I have met with Sigmund Adletsky and other members of the family to whom he recommended me and who wanted my advice, usually on matters of taste.

One thing I learned in my contacts with the old man: Wealth so profound can have no adequate human equivalent. He is very old now and small— light enough to fly away into the everlasting. His sons and grandsons, however, still report to him. His judgment in business matters, old style, is as sound as ever. The new world economy is unfamiliar to the founder. About his descendants, he once said to me, "I'm now in *their* brain trust."

Coming from a direction altogether different from Frances Jellicoe's or Sigmund Adletsky's is a person, a woman, whose name is Amy Wustrin. I briefly dated her in high school. Amy might or might not know the extent of the feelings that developed as a result of this hand holding, fondling, petting—the effects of this heady intimacy on me. It is of course impossible to guess what people know about one another.

When she was twelve or so, I watched her on roller skates—riding toward puberty. And in high school at fifteen at the annual Costume Day, when she wore tights and high heels, I saw her fully feminine thighs, the gloss and smoothness of sexual maturity on the cheeks and in the brown gaze: she transmitted messages of which she may not even have been aware.

Love object would be the commonest convenient term to indicate what Amy became to me. But where does that leave one? Suppose, instead of "love object," you were to say "door"—what sort of door? Does it have a knob; is it old or new, smooth or battered; does it lead anywhere? Half a century of feeling is invested in her, of fantasy, speculation, and absorption, of imaginary conversation. After forty years of concentrated imagining, I feel able to picture her at any moment of any given day. When she opens her purse to find her house keys, I am aware of the Doublemint chewing gum fragrance that comes out. When she is in the shower, I can tell you how she raises her profile to the spray. She's an older woman now. It's been thirty years since I saw her naked body, subject to the usual changes, like my own body—more Japanese than I would have thought, if Adletsky hadn't pointed it out.

But once, about a decade ago, I ran into Amy and failed to recognize her—the woman with whom I was virtually in daily mental contact. I ran into her at the edge of the Loop, under the Wabash Avenue el tracks. As I was passing she stopped me; she stepped in front of me and said, "Don't you know who I am?"

Though I can be brazen about ordinary social embarrassments, I felt that this was a very bad failure.

To her it was a terrific knock. She said, "You son of a bitch!" Meaning that if *I* didn't recognize her, she was no longer herself. She too, still presenting or, as we say, "selling" herself-as-she-used-to-be, was caught out in a falsehood.

"Who am I!" she said.

I shook my head. I *should* know who she was. But I didn't—I couldn't identify this enraged woman.

"Amy!" she said in a furious voice.

I saw her now. This was how it was. She was in the real world. I was not in it. "Hey, go easy, Amy," I said. "In all the time we've known each other, I've never run into you downtown. And under the el tracks when the weather is overcast, everything turns gray."

Because she was as gray-faced as a maid-of-all-work—an overworked mother. She had run out to do a quick errand, returning a pair of shoes her older daughter had changed her mind about. The thick, dried urban gumbo of dark Lake Street made everything look bad. Yes, she was unidentifiable below the black girders. Besides, her difficulties with her husband, Jay, were acute just then, and she feared she wasn't fit to be seen. Her looks were more mature. Or subdued. I'm looking for a tactful way to say it. Nobody comments on my changing appearance. My fat eyes and Chinese lips are the same. From the first, there was nothing to be got out of me.

But she knew how she had figured in my life and that I was in continual mental touch with her. I kept her preserved as she had been at fifteen years of age. So not to be identified when we were face-to-face must mean that she was in full ruin. I was shocked too.

I said to myself, "Edgewater 5340." That, in the

days before the numerical prefix, had been her phone number. She was, I think, the only girl I ever called on. I wasn't much of a wooer. When I rang at her front door, her mother seemed taken aback. I should have been the dry cleaner's messenger, picking up blouses.

But Amy had taken her raccoon coat from the hall tree and put on the matching round hat. She had a style of her own with hats—they were set back from her forehead. There are foreheads that can't tolerate the pressure of a hatband.

The house was not the usual brick. It was Indiana limestone. The porch was one thick slab of it. When Amy came out on the graystone porch, I inhaled her personal odor. Part of it was Coty's face powder. I ask myself whether Coty is still using the fragrance it used in the fifties. When we embraced and kissed in the park, the odor of the damp fur was much stronger than the powder.

The imperfect application of her lipstick was another point of identity. That was the whole power of it—the beauty of this flesh-and-blood mortality. Just as mortal was the shape of her bottom as she walked, a mature woman swinging a schoolbag. She didn't walk like a student. There was also the faulty management of her pumps. They dropped on the minor beat. This syncopation was the most telling idiosyncrasy of all. It bound the other traits together. What you were then aware of was the ungainly sexiness of her movements and her posture. The years between, with their crises and wars and presidential campaigns, all the transformations of the present age, have had no power to change her looks, the size of her eyes, or the brevity of her teeth. There's the power of Eros for you.

It's a March morning, then, on the fault line between cold and mild. A blizzard has burst, in a way peculiar to Chicago. The snow is going round and round, heavily, and Amy is in the tiled shower, soaping herself. The double cheeks of her backside are still well modeled, and she washes with the experienced hands of the mother who has bathed small children. A whole lifetime of self-care is apparent in the soaping of her breasts. Thirty years ago, I had the ecstatic privilege of lifting them up to kiss their undersides—and also the parted thighs.

Amy doesn't have the appearance of a woman who sets off such fantasies. There's a reserve about her that discourages a directly erotic approach. She seems very steady. She always has seemed so. At school she was an average sort in appearance. Except on Costume Day, in tights and lipstick like a showgirl. Young men like Jay, specialists at reading the sexual signs, guessed her to be excitable. "There's potential, there's action in that girl," he said. I was "going" with her, in our junior year, until Jay cut me out. They were married much later—after the Cuban missile crisis. A second marriage for both of them.

I was odd to look at. Not disagreeable, but neither was I to everyone's taste. Jay suited all tastes; he was an attractive man with a deliberate erotic emphasis in his looks.

But I must stay with her. At this moment she's turning off the shower, wondering how thick the snow will fall. This afternoon she has an errand at the cemetery, and a blizzard will make the expressway dangerous. And if the side streets are, as usual, choked in snow, she won't get through the endless neighborhoods—the bungalow belt. She has to go just over the city limits to—God help us!—the burial ground.

It had to be faced, however. Jay Wustrin, who had died the year before, was buried in Amy's family's plot. Behind this was a freakish mix-up, just the kind of screwball joke that appealed to the late Jay. He was a lawyer by profession, but he was also a comedian. In this matter, the comedian had prevailed, so that he now lay beside Amy's mother, who had disliked—no, hated—her daughter's husband. For all kinds of reasons, he had to be moved. There were obstacles to this move, bureaucratic problems with City Hall, with the Health Department. But the complicated legal work was finished at last. Jay Wustrin was scheduled to be moved this afternoon to another part of Waldheim

Cemetery. After endless paperwork, we were all set to go. She hadn't asked for my help. I say "we" because I was somehow involved, present or not present, on a parallel mental track. Amy avoided heavy feelings and perplexities. Coming out of the shower, frowning slightly, she worked her way around the problems of exhuming and reburial. As she wrapped herself in the towel, she prayed for a March storm to shut down the cemetery. The day was fuller already than she liked her days to be.

It would have amused Jay to cause so much trouble. You could rely on Amy to do the respectable thing. Her people were respectable, German-speaking Jews from Odessa, educated in a *gymnasium*. They had brought Amy up to *look* virtuous, and I suppose it's true that she had the appearance of a middle-class matron. Jay, by contrast, liked to think of himself and to see himself as a swinger. He chased women; he did very well at it, and he was handsome too, if your taste ran to conventional good looks—on the heavy side as he grew older. He and I had known each other as freshmen at Senn High School when I was an orphan—or non-orphan. We were close friends then. His father had owned a laundry. His mother distrusted me, for reasons I never bothered to think about. Jay and I read poetry together—T. S. Eliot, whom he called "*El*-yat," and Ezra Pound, whom he called "Pond." In his adolescence, he also admired Marie Stopes. Through him I was made familiar with *Married Love*. He was briefly a vegetarian and also a "post office socialist," arguing that all enterprises should be government run, just as the post office was. Later, very briefly, he was an anarchist. Through all these phases he was an *homme à femmes*. Women were his principal interest. Amy Wustrin was his second wife. I suppose he occasionally remembered that I had loved her at Senn, but the distant past didn't much matter to him. He must have forgotten it altogether, because when he was going with Amy, he invited me to join them at the Palmer House to shower together.

I asked, "Does she agree to this, or do you have a surprise in mind?"

"I'm not pulling any surprises. I've asked her," he said. "She just shrugged. 'Why not?'"

So I accepted, and we spent twenty minutes under the shower, the three of us. Early in the afternoon, he had to make a court appearance and left us two alone together. It was then that I kissed her under the breast and on the inner thigh. Afterward, it was terribly uncomfortable to think about our behavior in the shower—a radical discomfort that year after year became more acute.

Why did Jay set it up? Why did she consent? Why did I participate? I recall that when we were alone, she opened her mouth toward me, yearningly. But she didn't speak. Nor did I.

"I suppose Jay read about threesomes in some book. Havelock Ellis, maybe," I once said to her.

In the years following their marriage, I was a frequent dinner guest. Friend of the family.

After dinner he generally played classical records on the phonograph. And he presided over the concert—he put you through it with his extremely significant face. Especially the eyebrows. If it was *Don Giovanni*, he sang both Leporello and the Don. He had no ear at all, and yet he was more moved by it than anyone else. A strange cat, Jay indeed was.

Then, about five years before he died, Jay divorced Amy. The case he made against her was extremely ugly. "An open-and-shut adultery charge, and he slaughtered you," her lawyer said. "He doesn't have to give you a penny."

At that time Amy had no money of her own. Dead broke. Looking more than ever the middle-class matron in a tailored suit. She confessed, referring to that time, "I had to live in my aunt Dora's maid's room. Thank God both girls were away at school. Dora wasn't too glad to have me. She couldn't give me any money. When I put the house key in the lock, I heard her running to her room. I was looking in the lining of old purses for change, and I dug down in

the upholstered sofa for nickels and dimes. I owe it to
Jay that I learned what it means to be wiped out. I had
to learn to fight for life—a slug of disgrace was what
it took to make a battler out of me."

Amy's date this morning was with the old Adletskys. She had become an interior decorator.

Adletsky, never without his cellular telephone,
called Amy to say that he would be picking her up at
ten A.M. When he rang, on the dot, she went down.
The marquee outside her Sheridan Road apartment
house was warmed by glowing rods. A vast mid-
continental snow bag had burst over Chicago. The
flakes were very large. Adletsky's stretch limousine
was very slowly coming up through the snow,
lounging along the curb. The doorman stepped forward to open the door and hand Amy in. She took
her seat facing the two old people.

Old Mrs. Adletsky liked Amy. The matriarch,
too, was in her nineties, small and light—something
like a satin-wrapped pupa. Anything but dormant,
however. She had a crackling mind. And of course
she knew—she was bound to know—Amy's story.
Amy, thinking of the old woman's values, dated them
back to the beginning of the century. Mrs. Adletsky
would judge a woman's behavior by standards from
the days of Franz Josef and still more or less observed

by nonagenarians. Amy rightly considered that Mrs. Siggy's idea of a lady was the traditional one. But even these ancient trillionaires had to come to terms with things-as-they-were.

I have no dough, so it can't matter how dirty my private life is, Amy thought.

She was hard on herself. Her policy was to condition, to train herself not to give ground under the worst that could be said about her. Old Mrs. Adletsky had come to like her. She recommended her to friends. She would say, "You can trust this woman's taste, and she won't rip you off."

In the warm limousine, Adletsky was watching news and weather on three television sets. Dame Siggy, as some of the Adletsky staff, the personnel, referred to her, welcomed Amy with what Amy called her "from the next world" sweetness. Her bird legs, aslant, were laid together or set aside until they should be called upon to move. Her short fur jacket was thrown back. She was sipping her coffee as if there were no such thing as morning traffic on the Outer Drive.

"Good morning, Mrs. Adletsky. Good morning, Sigmund."

"Maybe today at last we can wrap up these negotiations with Heisinger."

The Adletskys were buying Heisinger's great duplex apartment on East Lake Shore Drive. The bargaining had gone on for two whole weeks.

Heisinger and his wife had insisted that the Adlet-skys buy their furniture. Amy's role was to appraise the value of the chairs, sofas, carpets, bedsteads, dressers—the drapes, even. "Of course, we have no use for their stuff," Dame Siggy said. "It'll go to the Michael Reese Hospital Thrift Shop, and we'll get the charitable IRS deduction."

Old Bodo Heisinger, not nearly so old as Adletsky—Amy estimated him to be in his mid-sixties—clearly felt challenged to hold his own as a moneyman against Siggy Adletsky. Heisinger, a successful toy manufacturer, had made things very hard for the buyers.

"I wish my wife hadn't set her heart on this joint," said old Adletsky. "What are we, young home-makers, starting out in life? But Florence just has to have it—to redecorate and so forth. It's a gorgeous view of the lake, sure enough. But as a bargainer this Bodo Heisinger takes himself much too seriously. Too much so . . ."

"He has to prove to *his* wife . . ."

"Oh, *his* wife. Of course he does. But he never will. He's frightened to death of her."

"She was one of Jay's clients, years ago," said Amy.

"I'm not surprised," said Adletsky. He seldom was genuinely surprised. He had never met Jay Wustrin. But in running a check on Amy, as such a man was bound to do, he had learned all he needed to know about her onetime husband. Jay was not a distinguished lawyer—he had no political clout, a serious disability in this city. He made intricate business passes that were foolish. His files were over-documented. It was a game with him to keep perfect records, but there wasn't all that much to record. The clients who kept him in business were old Northside neighbors, pals of his father. He drew their wills, and when they sold their houses he attended to the closings. I turned to him myself when I came back from Burma and Guatemala. If you had clear objectives and checked Jay's tendency to elaborate, to duplicate, and to triplicate, he could do your paperwork as well as another lawyer.

"What was the case?" said Adletsky.

"A former husband of hers," said Amy.

"A property matter?"

"Must have been. You *do* remember"—she changed the subject—"that I have a special chore this afternoon at the cemetery. Unless it can be called off because of the snowstorm."

"You can't count on that. There is no real blizzard. It's a wet snow that won't stick. According to the latest on TV, this weather system is bound for Michigan and Indiana."

"It's going to be blue sky and sunshine all afternoon," said Dame Siggy. "Wear boots; you'll need them out there."

"I'm not looking forward to it one bit."

"You've told me what this was about, and Quigley got you the permit to exhume the body." Quigley was one of Adletsky's staff of lawyers. "But it's still not clear why the man has to be moved."

It occurred to Amy that Adletsky wanted Dame Siggy to hear the particulars. And why not? The old woman—unnaturally old—lowered her face, listening, taking it all in.

"Your husband's coffin has to be dug up?"

"My parents bought graves in Waldheim many years ago, and after my mother died, my dad suddenly said he had no use for the space—his space. He started to say, 'What do I need this plot for? I'm going to sell it.' "

"How old was your father?"

"He's now eighty-one."

"And was he all there?"

"I can't say he was . . . or is."

"Gaga? But not Alzheimer's . . . ?"

"It didn't have to be Alzheimer's. He got the fixed idea of selling his grave, he came back to it day after day, and for some reason he insisted that Jay should buy it. That's my late husband, Mrs. Adletsky."

"I've gathered that."

"Jay enjoyed that sort of joke. He used to tease my dad and say, 'Don't you want to be buried next to your wife—the two of you forever and ever?' And my father would answer, 'No, I'd rather have the money. It's foolish. For me it doesn't make sense to keep it. What do I need it for! You buy it from me.' Jay said, 'Won't you be jealous if I'm beside her?' And he'd tell him, 'It's not in my character to be jealous. I haven't got a jealous nature.' "

"And your old dad is still living?"

"Oh, yes. In a retirement home."

"But he got his way?"

"Yes. It was a terrific story for Jay to tell. I didn't want any part of it. Jay said, 'I'll do it just to stop the old guy from bugging me.' I objected, but my objection didn't count, and finally Jay wrote my father a check and there was a legal transfer of title. Jay had no idea that my father would outlive him. A few years later we were separated, and then divorced—"

"And your husband went downhill . . . ," said Adletsky.

"Gave up his law practice, lost his health. Fell back on the little estate inherited from his mother, which wasn't much to begin with. While in the hospital, he asked to see me, and I went there. I spent time with him. . . . What was his trouble?" she said, responding to the question on Dame Siggy's sharp uplifted face. "He had a cardiac insufficiency. His lungs filled up."

"So when he died . . . ?" Adletsky led Amy toward a conclusion.

The great polished concert-piano limousine had left the Drive. Through the tinted windows, nothing identifiable could be seen.

"His children found the title to the grave in Jay's bank box, and they buried him beside Mother."

"But you will need that space . . . ?"

"Shortly, I think."

"It can't be left till after the fact," said Mrs. Adletsky.

"Do Wustrin's children object to moving him?"

"Not if it doesn't cost them," said Amy. "They agreed to the move on that condition."

"Can your father recognize you when you come to visit?"

"Not often. His mental pictures keep changing."

Geometric scrawls of light, as on a TV screen.

Dame Siggy didn't wish to dwell on the father. She was about to buy a new apartment and to furnish and redecorate. As if she were a bride. "What a sense of humor your late husband had," she said.

Jay did like to be publicly seen performing, entertaining, innovating. A stout man, dancing, he swung his broad backside, but his feet were very agile. Neat enough to be called deft. At school he used to do Dr. Jekyll turning into Mr. Hyde, shining a flashlight into his face. Just like the movies. John Barrymore, was it, or his brother, Lionel? Or Lon

Chaney, the great contortionist who played Quasimodo in *The Hunchback of Notre Dame*.

"Transferring a coffin to another grave all by your lonesome?" said Dame Siggy. "Isn't there anybody to go with you—a friend, or one of your children?"

"One of my daughters is married, in New York. The younger is a student in Seattle, at the university."

Adletsky agreed with his wife. "You should have a helping hand."

The marquee of the Heisingers' apartment was sheltered from the blasting wind by walls of canvas. They entered the regal elevator. The gilded ceiling suggested a Byzantine chapel; the walls were quilted leather. The Adletskys sat down together on a cushioned seat. A silent elevator man brought them to the sixteenth floor, and the brass gate, rows of diamond shapes, noiselessly came open. There Bodo Heisinger, compact and serious, stood waiting. He was dressed in a business suit. When he moved, you were surprised to see that he was wearing carpet slippers. He shook hands with the old people and nodded to Amy. There are trillionaires, and then there are supernumeraries, Amy silently observed.

"Mrs. Wustrin is here to take notes toward an appraisal," Adletsky said.

He spoke with a trace of an accent, but his business English was very good.

"If you feel you have to have your own appraiser," said Heisinger. He had led them to a room looking over the lake—hundreds of miles of water opening beyond the gray snow cloud. There was a round gaming table: Irish, eighteenth century—Amy had checked it out—green leather with a gilt border. This was one of the few genuinely good pieces. Heisinger had chosen for tactical reasons to work his way toward a closing in this room. The rest of the inventory—Amy had gone over it with her Merchandise Mart experts—amounted to very little.

"My wife will join us by and by," said Bodo Heisinger. He chatted, filling up the time.

Old Adletsky listened unmoved. When Bodo announced that his wife was coming, it was the ladies who were interested—Amy most of all. Dame Siggy had already met the problematic Mrs. Heisinger. Because she *was* problematic. More than that, Madge Heisinger was a notorious woman. Her husband had divorced her and then married her again. Jay Wustrin, when he represented Mrs. Heisinger earlier, in an unrelated legal matter, had told Amy that she had made a real impression on him. He came home from the office smiling and said, describing or trying to describe her, "She makes no bones about it—she's a real nihilist. She tells you so herself."

Dame Siggy had told Amy that Mrs. Heisinger wore Escada suits and Nina Ricci dresses. "She acts very provocative," the old woman added.

Well, if Mrs. Heisinger was provocative, she would have provoked Jay. That would have suited him just fine. She might have had a smaller legal bill to pay than a less exciting client. (She wasn't married to Bodo Heisinger then, and money might have been a consideration.) Jay's clients often were problem women—nihilists, if you prefer, his favorite term. The excitement such women brought into his office meant much more to him than fees. If being sexual was like being drunk, Jay was something like a drunken driver.

Then I stopped being of any real interest to him, Amy was thinking, pulling the skirt of her blue knitted suit toward her knees. She had observed this early in the marriage. This morning Amy wore a good deal of makeup, especially around the eyes, where it was most needed. Her round face was calm, though her inner reckoning machines ran at high speed. Age sometimes brings slovenliness to women of a full build. But it was plain that she was still in control of her appearance; her traits and faculties were rounded up—they were on view in the corral. She was a beauty, her skin still smooth; she even breathed like a beauty.

If she had been my wife—not Mrs. Jay Wustrin but Mrs. Harry Trellman—her very body, in her early fifties, might have looked . . . no, would have *been* different. I could have offered her accommodations of a mental, imaginative sort.

At the moment, sitting in the warm penthouse, the last of the snow scattering as the weather system crossed the lake, strong air currents from the west clearing the two vast blues of air and water, Amy and the Adletskys were waiting for Mrs. Heisinger to appear. What Bodo Heisinger was saying was that Madge was concerned about the appraisal of the furniture. It just wouldn't do. She had bought the sofas, chairs, breakfronts, carpets, hangings, mirrors, paintings, in the best shops, mainly at the Merchandise Mart, and with no decorators to guide her. She had kept all the bills.

Mr. Adletsky, very low-keyed, said, "Ten years ago, or even fifteen?"

Certainly, said Bodo Heisinger, but the value of the antiques, like this beautiful Irish gaming table, had doubled.

"We have your appraisal. Mrs. Wustrin is preparing hers."

In the guide to great fortunes published in Austin, Texas, Adletsky was ranked well above Malcolm Forbes and Turner of CNN, whereas Bodo Heisinger did not appear at all. In the old days he had manufactured squirt guns, peashooters, wind-up she-monkeys who combed their monkey hair while jiggling a hand mirror—nowadays, of course, children wanted hideous outer-space aliens, monstrously muscled and distorted. He had anticipated this, and his company was doing extremely well. It was tolerant of Adletsky to let Bodo play the great capitalist. The sums named were as trivial to the Adletskys as change slipping from your pants pocket between the sofa cushions and down into the upholstery.

Dame Siggy may have been concerned lest Heisinger carry things too far. She had set her heart on the apartment, and there was no reason why she shouldn't have it, a woman of such wealth. But Bodo was beginning to bore Adletsky. Irritation would come next. He was quite capable of standing up and asking coldly for his hat and coat.

Well, perhaps when he was younger, in the days when the fortune was being founded, Adletsky had been an imperious sorehead, angry, impatient, intolerant. I had the impression that he was now much more temperate. There were reasons for Heisinger's "negotiating stance," of which Adletsky was aware. Even a remote business titan, simply because he lived here, couldn't help knowing. It had all been reported by the papers and on the air. Madge Heisinger was the criminal wife, convicted of trying to have the elderly toy manufacturer killed.

Some weeks before all this, Adletsky had discussed the history of the case with me. I was no longer his brain truster and on the payroll. By now I was running a very profitable business. I had stopped accepting his fee. But I was pretty well up on the matters that had begun to interest him—human matters. And it was plain to him that the woman he referred to as "your very good friend Mrs. Wustrin," or "your protégé," held a special place in my feelings. It may have seemed curious to him that a man like me should *have* such feelings for anyone. He had once or twice said to me, "I don't take you for an emotional heavyweight. But all that means is that I missed something when I sized you up. We are both oddball Jews, Harry. But I founded this considerable fortune, which it so happens is a very Jewish thing."

I agreed, with a significant shrug, and he took this thought no further.

"But about the Heisingers ... I was away during the trial," said Adletsky.

"Five or six years ago, she put out a contract on her husband; the hit man was somebody she knew from way back—a man she used to go with long before," I explained to him.

"Did he hurt him at all?"

"I think not. Bodo knocked the gun out of his hand. The guy ran. There were prints on the pistol. The police identified this person, and he incriminated Madge Heisinger."

"So she was convicted?"

"Both were, and did three years. . . ."

"They were paroled?"

"Yes. Heisinger withdrew his complaint. He wanted Madge back. . . ."

"He's got to be one of those men who dote on problem women," said Adletsky.

"He married her a second time. One of the conditions she made was that the hit man go free too. She couldn't be happy while he was doing time. She promised not to resume relations with him."

"So they married a second time and started all over, as good as new."

"To Heisinger it must seem daring—like an innovation," I said. "Like the distinguished twist in a relationship. A man free from general opinions."

"About what?"

"Oh, about gullibility, age, or potency. He opens his arms again to the woman who put out a contract on him. He presents himself publicly to declare that he's not afraid to marry her again, and he sets aside the old morality and the old expectations and old rules."

Amy thought that Bodo somewhat resembled Jay, her ex, her late husband. Both felt that nihilism was sexy and seemed to believe that there was no real eroticism that didn't defy the taboos. Neither Jay nor old Heisinger was sharply intelligent. Very sexy men frequently were stupid, and shared stupidity is an important force when it is presented in the language of independence or emancipation. The appeal of such men is aimed straight at those strata in women's feelings that lie beneath cleverness. The strength of a Heisinger was his blunt masculinity. He was straightforward and stout, elderly but in the running still—not afraid of being tested. He showed, or tried to show, that he was not worried about the jailbird boyfriend. The boyfriend had been punished, Madge had been punished. Everybody had been tortured. Amy, trying to get into Bodo's mind, felt that he was thinking of the time remaining, a decade or so: "the final years," as biographers refer to them—a period of "mature" acceptance, reconciliation, openhandedness, general amnesty. She suspected that Heisinger was too limited a man to understand how wrong he might be. Jay, too, had worked out glamorous projects that nobody else was able to accept—scenarios too histrionic to be translated into real terms.

As well as I could, I spelled this out to Adletsky. He had no difficulty with it. It was exactly this that he wanted to hear from Trellman, his brain truster. He was an intent critical listener.

If there were parallels between Bodo Heisinger and Jay Wustrin, would there be resemblances also between their wives? Amy anticipated that there might be *some*. Of course, Heisinger was a millionaire many times over. Jay Wustrin's father had left some money, but Jay managed it badly. He was clumsy with banks, interest rates, investments. His mother outlived her husband by twenty-five years, and although she kept her expenses down for Jay's sake, living like a pauper, in the end Jay had had to support her.

I knew the mother well; she didn't care for me; she believed I was an undesirable friend for Jay, self-serving—the orphan on whom Jay spent his allowance. When we were adolescents and boxed in the alley (the gloves were his), Mrs. Wustrin held it against me that I would hit Jay in the face.

"But I punch Harry just as often. . . ."

She would shake her big brainless head at him. Jay was embarrassed by his mother. With her rich, stupid black eyes, much like her son's, she was nevertheless a handsome woman. Her family had sold her, more or less, to old Wustrin, many years her senior. He had put her to work in his laundry. She was passive, thick-headed, devoted to Jay, her only child. Maybe it wasn't stupidity her black eyes showed, but arrested sexuality. An old-country village woman, she mapped careers for her son. He would be a famous lawyer, earning millions and making speeches reported in the papers. Like Clarence Darrow. But Jay was a ladies' man. Perhaps even his blockhead mother was aware of this.

I see myself taking pleasure in these assorted people, their motives, their behavior. Only one of them do I genuinely care about. I've had imaginary meetings and conversations with Amy several times a week for years now. In these mental discussions we have reviewed all the errors I made—scores of them—the worst being my failure to pursue, to compete for, her.

She might have said, "Where the hell have you been all our life?"

A good question!

But that's not exactly what I have in mind just now. It's the others I'm thinking of: Bodo Heisinger, Madge Heisinger, and, in spite of their vast wealth, the Adletskys. And of Amy's senile father, the fantasist who had unloaded his own grave on his son-in-law.

Jay had bought his father-in-law's plot for the fun of it. It gave him an amusing story to tell at his Standard Club lunches.

These were all commonplace persons. I would never have let them think so, but it's time to admit that I looked down on them. They were lacking in higher motives. They were run-of-the-mill products of our mass democracy, with no distinctive contribution to make to the history of the species, satisfied to pile up money or seduce women, to copulate, thrive in the sack as the degenerate children of Eros, male but not manly, and living, the men and women alike, on threadbare ideas, without beauty, without virtue, without the slightest independence of spirit—privileged in the way of money and goods, the beneficiaries of man's conquest of nature as the

Enlightenment foresaw it and of the high-tech achievements that have transformed the material world. Individually and personally, we are unequal to the scope of these collective achievements.

But although I had such feelings and made such judgments, I couldn't rid myself of the habit of watching for glimpses of higher capacities and incipient powerful forces in, say, the rich, stupid black eyes of Jay Wustrin's mother, or in Bodo Heisinger's second try—his marriage to the wife jailed for plotting to have him rubbed out, knocked off, shot dead.

I myself seem to be doing an idiotic thing in looking for signs of highest ability in human types evidently devoted to being barren.

Sometimes I wonder whether my mother, whom I have long suspected of being a hypochondriac, had done this to me by putting me into a Jewish orphanage, where I was taught (but at the time did not agree) that the Jews were a chosen people. This may be the nucleus of my belief that the powers of our human genius are present where one least expects them. Yes, even in what a friend of mine once described as "the moronic inferno."

I don't claim one single thing for this (personal) habit of examining features and behaviors. It's all intuited. Not a thing is provable. And very possibly it is a carryover from some vestigial Jewish impulse, in some instances still strongly at work.

With my Chink or Jap looks, I am seldom taken for a Jew. I suppose there is some advantage in this. When you are identified as a Jew, you are fair game. The rules of behavior change, and you become in a sense expendable. Now, Adletsky, as one of the richest men in the world, didn't need to care whether you esteemed him or not. He was openly Jewish, because it was altogether too clear. Besides, your opinion didn't matter a damn to him. But the case of Bodo Heisinger was different. You couldn't say whether or not Bodo was a Jew. Would a Jew divorce and then marry again a woman convicted of scheming to murder him? To do that put him far beyond any Jewish conception of the relations between men and women.

The old toy manufacturer needed to be where the action was, all the kinks and the scandals. He still drove his mental motorcycle and drove, as it were, at top speed along the rim of the Grand Canyon. He had knocked the hit man's gun out of his hand. He had had him put away. And then he had had him released. When the kids' demand was for ever more repulsive, menacing space-alien dolls, he anticipated the trend and led the industry in sales.

And, now, in came Madge. Amy remembered having met her once or twice when she was Jay's client, fifteen years ago. She looked different—very attractive, Amy granted. She was slender, not too hippy. Prison must have kept her in condition. She had a good bust, an oval face, a well-shaped head. She was very fair, a golden babe whose hair was pinned tightly, almost to the point of strain, and braided at the back. Amy had seen her silk suit in an Escada window—five thousand bucks on her back, plus matching sapphires on the fingers and hanging from her ears. The few golden hairs that broke loose from control seemed independently strong. In the wilderness (Amy allowed herself a fun image), you could make a trout fly of such hairs and attach it to a bent pin. In jail for forty months, she had probably worn dungarees or smocks. But now there wasn't a shadow of prison anywhere. Merely a change of scene and costume. She was very handsome, Amy thought. It was only the woman's nose that was wrong—too full at the tip to be entirely feminine. All the more reason, therefore, to present the volup- tuous bust in an Escada frame. She wore a silk blouse with ruffled cuffs. This Madge Heisinger was a real turn-on. Imagine what an effect she would have made lying nude, wearing nothing but the sap- phires, drawing a man toward her with salty sweet- talk. Plus (let's not omit it) the extra relish of a plotted murder.

Bodo the intended murderee was tremendously proud of her. And of himself, an aged manufacturer and worldwide distributor of muscular, horrendous, laser-armed space aliens for small boys and girls. He was now affirming to press and television how strong his love was. And declaring for the record that he, too, was a subversive, not a bourgeois but a nihilist, part of the "counterculture," in (or almost in) with the criminal class. Again I saw parallels between Bodo and Jay Wustrin, my friend from childhood. It had always meant much to them to be looked up to by women.

I suppose it had occurred to Madge—in jail, where she had plenty of time to think—that Bodo hadn't many years to live and that it hadn't been necessary to put out a contract on him. Then he wrote to say that he could arrange to have her released—he wanted her back.

Well, here she was, being agreeable to the Adletskys while studying Amy in side glances.

Was it a blizzard? No, it wasn't. Only a snow squall. The water brightened as the sky cleared.

Amy was round-eyed, soft-cheeked, with a slight hook to the nose. Those eyes in a somewhat flattened face at times gave her a silly look. Such would certainly be Madge's summary.

"So you're Mrs. Wustrin. Your late husband— excuse me, ex-husband—handled a legal matter for me long ago."

"I think we had dinner together at Les Nomades," said Amy.

"Yes, come to think of it. And now you've made a name for yourself as a decorator. . . ."

"Yes. Mr. and Mrs. Adletsky retained me to do an estimate of your things."

"This stuff is all top quality. The Chinese pieces are genuine, authenticated by Gump's of San Francisco. Our adviser on some purchases was Dick Erdman—"

Adletsky said, "I'm not going to involve myself with the inflated fees paid to professional decorators like Erdman. If your pieces are so wonderful, you should keep them. My wife will refurnish to her own taste."

Madge worked her painted fingers, as if to rid them of some invisible thread or stickiness. "In a case like yours, Mr. Adletsky—"

"I'm an intending buyer and you're the seller. Never mind my case. That's all there is to the deal."

"Yes, but we don't start from scratch," said Madge. "We're not exactly anonymous parties."

"What do you mean—that we're all in the papers? That your furniture will become a conversation item? Like the Kennedy auction? We're not interested in buying topics to talk about."

Madge crossed her arms and walked back and forth. She was extremely restless. She went between the glass doors, passing into the long living room as if she were inspecting the sofas, the settees,

and the Persian carpets, putting something of herself into them again. Something sexual? Something
criminal? She asserted her significance. She wasn't
about to let you forget it. She spread, she scattered,
she sprinkled it. She hadn't done time for nothing.
When I met her, she made me think of a course
in field theory, and I mean psychological field
theory—for which I registered in my student
days—having to do with the mental properties
of a mental region under mental influences that
resembled gravitational forces. Adletsky, however,
was not about to grant her any field. There was
many a corporate executive, a Treasury official, and
more than one foreign prime minister with anecdotes to relate about Adletsky's total refusal to
accept the other party's bargaining premises.

"You must allow for the losses we have to
take," said Bodo. He was holding a folder stuffed
with documents.

"Minus a few items we reserve for ourselves,"
said Madge. "We value our things at a million and a
half. I'm bringing it down from two." She gripped her
arms even more tightly. High up, close to the top of
her shoulder, she held a cigarette.

Adletsky said the seller, Heisinger, was giving
himself a bonus, getting back what he had conceded
in the bargaining. "Since Mrs. Heisinger has intro-
duced personal considerations as adding value to

these chairs and sofas, may I as well say that for me, in my nineties, if I don't make this purchase I'll make another one. I'm not of an age to set my heart on a specific acquisition. Dame Siggy and I are okay, perfectly comfortable where we are."

Madge's posture was becoming slightly rigid across the shoulders. She backed up her head and made you feel that she was responding to a drop in the temperature of the room. "Mrs. Adletsky will be happy here," she said. "You probably could talk her out of it, but she's already fitting herself into these gorgeous rooms."

A Mexican couple now entered to serve tea and coffee, silent Indians. The woman wore a hanging braid. The man's face was wide and brown, coppery, flattened at the top, black cropped hair glittering. He put down the big silver tray, and his wife set out the cups and plates. Madge sent away the servants and did the pouring.

Mrs. Adletsky preferred tea.

"Some of the same for me, please," said Amy when Madge turned to her. She held up her cup. Madge turned aside the spout and poured hot tea into Amy's lap.

"I'm scalded," said Amy loudly. She stood up.

"Oh, what a clumsy jerk I am," said Madge. Stern toward herself, she spoke through her nose as though there were no one else in the room.

Adletsky offered Amy his napkin.

"Are you burned?" said Madge.

"I was better before," said Amy. "Lucky I'm wearing this thick tweed."

"How dumb of me. I should have put in my contacts."

"Contacts!" said Amy later, describing the moment. "I could have put both her eyes out then and there."

"If there's any Unguentine in the house, you should put some on," said old Dame Siggy.

"Or aloe vera—even better," said Bodo. "We keep an aloe plant in the kitchen."

"If you'll direct me to the bathroom," said Amy.

"I'll take you there myself," said Madge. "The least I can do."

As they hurried out, Bodo the happy narcissist watched with benevolence from his hollow face. "They say the aloe vera has to be three years old to take the sting out of a burn. A young plant doesn't do it," Bodo explained.

Madge moved quickly, Amy more slowly, fighting her rage and preparing her words. . . . This was no accident. Not a drop of the tea went into the cup. You sure learned a thing or two in the slammer. But you're back in civilian life, it's time you realized. We're not behind bars.

Amy, with an angry face, denounced the gaudy

rooms. They were disgusting, decorated with a heavy hand by Dick Whatchumacallum and his male team, all wearing Armani costumes. Hip huggers.

Madge turned toward Amy with a quite pleasant, even friendly smile. And now Amy saw that Bodo Heisinger was coming from the other end of the corridor; he held up a piece of aloe vera. This would have amused her if she had been less angry. Madge took the green stalk and sent Bodo back to the Adletskys. The bathroom lights went on. "You're not coming in with me," Amy said, and forced her aside. She observed that Madge was smiling at her and seemed more pleased than not by Amy's show of temper.

As she shut the door against Madge and turned the lock, Amy was obliged to admit that she had not been seriously burned. To have tea poured deliberately into her lap was nevertheless an outrage. And then for the woman to try to push her way into the bathroom, as not even a sister would do after you had come of age. It made Amy consider: sane or insane? There must be some degree of privacy even in a women's prison. If the woman *was* sane, she was getting more mileage than she should out of the time she had served. Madge took every pretext to set aside the lady conventions. And there were no reasons to assume that she was clinically bonkers. High-handed, a bully, and perhaps when you were a convict you picked up some masculine ways. But that didn't add up to insanity.

The Heisinger bathroom, too, was overdeco-
rated—too many thick towels, too many appliances.
Amy couldn't see frail old Mrs. Adletsky in the
crimson Jacuzzi—she'd be swept away. Beside the
bath was a toilet with a cushioned cover on the lid,
and Amy pulled down her underclothes and had
seated herself, when Madge came in. She entered
from the master bedroom. The toilet was in a recess
between the whirlpool bath and a shower stall. Amy
had failed to notice how long the tiled room actually
was. Beyond, there were washbasins and mirror
walls, and there was a dressing room as well.

"I don't think I was especially well brought up,"
said Amy, "but I was taught that this is one place
where privacy is respected."

"Well, I gave you time enough to examine the
burned spot. The tea was lukewarm, not boiling. The
Mexicans do good coffee, but they don't understand
how to brew tea. I realized when I poured the old
lady her cup that it was tepid. I wanted a private talk,
to have you to myself awhile. That was the whole
idea. Wasn't it sweet of Bodo to bring the aloe vera?
It's one of his special remedies. But I can see for
myself that the red scald isn't too bad. You got wet,
I'm sorry to say, and I'll pay the cleaner's bill too, but
tea won't stain—we used to rub spots out with tea
when I was young."

"Well, let me pull my clothes into place."

"Yes, adjust a little, honey, and don't mind me."

"You did behave like a wild bitch," said Amy. "Do you always do every goddamn thing that rushes into your head?"

"Well, at least I didn't set you up for a hit."

"She joked about trying to set up Heisinger," Amy said to me later.

"I understand your getting sore. But I take you for the kind of woman who might see the fun side of it."

"Of tea poured in my lap?"

"I already explained why. It did happen kind of fast, I admit, and I acted on it as soon as it came into my thoughts. It rushed in, just as you said. But it was also kind of a comment. You looked like such a damn matron."

"How would you look with scratches on your face?"

"That's nothing but talk. You'd queer yourself with the Adletskys. It pays you to be on your best ladylike behavior. That Dame Siggy can make you popular as a decorator in her social set of billionaires. How would it look if I went back with toilet tissue on the scratch? . . . Just a moment, till I get the little stool out of the shower stall."

She draped the light plastic seat in a towel and leaned back against the wall. The tiles were shining their damnedest.

"Why do we have to talk in the toilet? Why not your boudoir?"

"It's more basic in here. You'll dry quicker if I turn up the heat and the fan. You may want to take off your things and hang them over the vent."

"I'll stay as I am."

"Suit yourself. . . . How big an estimate will you give on the furnishings?"

"You won't think it's high enough."

"There's not one single cheap item in the whole house."

"Are you proposing that I should jack up the appraisal? I'd have a fat chance of misleading a person as sharp as Mr. Adletsky."

"Of course, a top, superpower billionaire. Besides, you could never do anything dishonest," said Madge. "You're one of those ladies who maintain a heavy honest image."

"This sounds like the view of the outside you'd hear from convicts. It's general opinion by now, in or out of jail, and it runs like this: 'If the facts were known, people behind bars are no guiltier than people outside, because nobody is clean, and only people inside know what's real and what's phony.' I suppose you have to make the most of, or get what advantages you can out of the time you served."

Madge Heisinger made no reply. She might have been weighing her options, and in the end she decided not to take Amy up on this. She said, "I liked Jay Wustrin. . . . He wasn't a brainy lawyer. He came on strong—I can tell what you're thinking—but all we had was a business relationship, strictly. I laid out the strategy in my case, and he did the paperwork. Well, he's dead now. How long has it been?"

"About eight months."

"I attended the service for him. I don't recall that you were there," said Madge.

"I couldn't make it."

"A few months before he passed away, I had lunch with him. He was no longer his handsome self. Not just his health was bad. He was generally in terrible shape. There was a bad smell from his clothes, his teeth weren't clean, and when he tried to do the charm smile he used to do, that deliberate lift of his upper lip, it was a failure. He said he stopped practicing law a year ago."

"More like three years," said Amy. "He spent his time around the Michigan Avenue bookshops. He had unpaid bills there, and he wasn't welcome. And the customers didn't want to hear him quoting his favorite poets. This went back to our school days. He memorized bits to recite when he was putting the make on girls. After we were married, I looked up all his source books. The passages were underlined, and just from Chapter One. He never read an entire book in his whole life. Here is a sample: 'The face

of man is the most amazing thing in the life of
the world. Another world shines through it. It is the
entrance of personality into the world process, with
its uniqueness, its unrepeatability. Through the face
we apprehend, not the bodily life of a man, but
the life of his soul.' One of his favorite Russians
said that. When we were dating, he repeated this as
his own."

"He knew better than to lay such shit on me,"
said Madge. "Who wrote it?"

"Underlined with a ruler, in red. Just Chapter
One. The rest he never looked at."

"Pretty tricky."

"Pretending to be an intellectual, for purposes
of seduction. Like an item from *Playboy*. Coaching
young men on how to weave the web."

"But you memorized those words yourself."

"I did do it, didn't I?"

"Well, the last time I saw him, it was clear that
he was going, going, gone," said Madge. "There was
only one interest in his life, and he had to give that
up. So it was time to leave. That was when he turned
weak and gentle. I was sorry to see him on the skids.
He spoke intimately. . . ."

As soon as she said "intimately," Amy knew all
too well what Madge was about to get at: Jay had
told her about the tapes.

"The evidence against me, well, he had me dead

to rights," said Amy. "So don't feel too privileged. He played those tapes to everybody who would listen to them. What he had done was to hire an agency. He gave them a key to the apartment. That's how it was set up. The specialists bugged my phone for months. Even the bed was bugged. There were microphones in the mattress. All this evidence was played in chambers for the judge. Jay made the perfect adultery case against me. . . ."

Amy had become all too familiar with the expression she saw on Madge's face. She had seen it in others—a sidelong, oblique look of amusement, appearing on the half-averted cheek.

"Yes, he told me about this," said Madge. "And did I want to listen to the evidence?"

"And you did want to listen?"

"Well, I was just out of a correctional facility. You don't see newspapers there. Television, yes, but no *Tribune*. It makes you feel how much behind you are, how much you've missed."

"Our divorce was hardly at all in the papers," said Amy. "This was why Jay grabbed the opportunity to play the tapes to anybody ready to listen. I wouldn't say that it was revenge exclusively. . . ."

"How much it hurt him is understandable," Madge said. It was only mischief, nothing like arranging to have Bodo put down in the underground garage.

Madge added, "I suppose, in your social circle,

it made you look bad—those cries and moans and raunchy talk."

Amy could hear the rush of blood under her skull. When it descended to her face, she felt the roughness of it. Her mouth went dry. "So he watched your reactions while you listened on the headphones?"

"About ten minutes of it, only," said Madge.

Amy thought: She now classes us together. We're two of a kind, she and I, and both publicly exposed. My scandal; her trial lasting for weeks. Together we make a double bill.

Amy spelled this out for me, to the extent possible—all the immediate circumstances, down to the cushioned toilet-lid cover, the soaked lap of her skirt, and the fan-driven flood of tropical heat in the long bathroom.

"According to the deal I made with Bodo, I get to keep the furniture money—whatever the old people pay for it. . . . I can't bear to look at those dressers anymore, and the love seats. These were my surroundings for ten terrible years. They maybe drove me to that stupid scheme. Just looking, day in, day out, at those fucking things made me not only heavyhearted and gut sick, but finally mental."

"Adletsky will never pay an extra million for your apartment," said Amy. "It's not so easy to put the arm on a billionaire. Don't expect him to hand out money. He'd sooner walk away from the sale altogether."

"If she wants to play at being young and starting out in life, he should let her. What's money to him? The dough is not for me. It's for Tommy Bales," Madge said.

"Who?" said Amy. But she quickly placed the name. Tommy Bales was the incompetent freak who agreed to do the hit on Bodo Heisinger. . . . "What about Tommy Bales?"

"I have to do something of a practical nature to make it up to him for the three years he lost in the slammer, plus a year of waiting for trial. And he wasn't going anywhere before that. So now I plan to set him up in business. That's another thing I wanted your opinion on—your help, to be frank."

This appeal for frankness will have to be set aside for the moment.

What did it mean that Adletsky and Dame Siggy had reached a great age, that they were honored as multibillionaire Jews, and that they were what Chicagoans call "notables"? Or else, in the language of myth, "heavy-money Yids," representatives of the powers of darkness and the secret rulers of the world?

Much later in the day, talking to Amy about Mr. and Mrs. Adletsky, I said, "Okay, they're in retirement. They've got nothing but leisure, and it's a pastime with them to bargain with Bodo Heisinger, to chaffer and haggle. Early this morning, they left the house and rode downtown through the blizzard in their stretch limo. They sat in the luxurious salon interior. Then for two hours they fenced with Madge and Bodo. . . . There was no occasion to look outside—to see the people whose mad doings the papers are always reporting. . . ."

"What are you out to prove, Harry, with an introduction like this?" Amy said.

"There is no leisure for anybody," I said. "Retirement is an illusion. Not a reward but a mantrap. The bankrupt underside of success. A shortcut to death. Golf courses are too much like cemeteries. Adletsky would never stoop to golf. He was right to wheel and deal as he had done from the age of two till ninety-two."

This sort of speculation had always made Amy uncomfortable. I was already talking like this in high school. She didn't really listen. She saw this as one of my bad habits, and maybe she was right. My theorizing had from the beginning come between us. "You aren't really the way you sound," she sometimes said. "You've read so many books, but surprisingly, face-to-face you aren't bookish—you're regular."

Berner, her first husband, by whom she had had two daughters, had made no theoretical statements. He was a gambler. As a young wife, she went with him to football games in Soldier Field, to hockey at the stadium. "I enjoyed it," she said. "Not your kind of thing, Harry. You're a university type—you're studious, you don't look like a highbrow but you are one." She didn't like me to claim superiority. On the other hand, I was an oddball, she said. I looked so curiously self-contained. "You never let on to more than one-tenth of what you really think or know. You used to be a Marxist. Weren't you, for a while? What ever happened to the book you wrote on What's-his-name . . . ?"

"On Walter Lippmann. Nobody would take it. It never was published."

Berner, whom she married when she got her B.A., inherited a small raincoat factory. He gambled it away. He took a bank loan on the house in Oak Park, and soon Amy and her girls were homeless. Berner disappeared for a good while. She obtained a divorce. The children were still quite young when she married Jay Wustrin.

"Berner didn't even abandon us," she said. "He barely noticed that we were there."

"He didn't need to have a family. He only needed to desert one. I fail to see how it was possible to leave you, Amy. You were a great beauty."

"To you, maybe. But not even to you. You didn't come to court me."

"I was married myself just then."

"Maybe so. But that didn't keep *your* wife from wandering."

"No. And I was a strictly faithful husband for a dozen years. . . . I loved you, Amy," I said. This had a ponderous sound. I felt, speaking in this way, like a piece of pottery—a large crockery jar. To speak of love made me clumsy. It turned my thoughts toward my mother, whom I disliked. I couldn't forgive her for putting me in an orphanage while she traveled from spa to spa. She limped, it's true. The disability was real enough. She walked with a stick. But the difficulties were not wholly physical. On the trains, her rich brothers, my sausage-maker uncles, always reserved a drawing room for her. The trouble was that it bored her to be the wife of a simple working stiff. To top it all, I resemble her, except in point of color. I have a somewhat Mongolian and tawny complexion. She was always very pale. She coiled her hair, wore it high on her head. Her cheeks were large and soft. Her nose looped inward. I inherited her prominent lips. Taken item by item, her features were not attractive, yet she did have an attractive and even a distinguished face—like a very fine Tartar woman with an unusually white complexion. In her generation, women with intellectual interests wore a pince-nez. One dangled from her fragrant neck.

Another characteristic in common: my mother

kept her own counsel. It gave me an incomprehensible satisfaction to deny almost everyone access to my thoughts and opinions. People always were willing to confide in me, though I didn't ever encourage confidences. I said very little of a personal nature. Except to Amy Wustrin.

We had, let's say, a score of years remaining. One should probably write off the final five—make a reasonable allowance for ailments. That left fifteen fully worth having.

I was prepared by now to make my peace with my species. For most of them, I am aware in hindsight, I generally had a knife within reach.

In the last phase of maturity, one could, one should, be straight with oneself.

"If you were faithful to a distant, cold woman," said Amy, "Jay wasn't at all, to me, when I was doing my best."

I used to wonder about this. Jay and I were friends from the age of twelve, and he never failed to tell me whose wife he was sleeping with. On New Year's Eve, he invited all these unfaithful women, past and present, to the annual party the Wustrins gave. While I was chatting with a victim-husband, Jay would pass behind the man, signaling with his eyebrows. That the facts should be known was essential. And they had to be registered by me in particular. My opinion mattered to him, and he even lectured me, tried to teach me his own view—the correct view—of himself. He said I was behind the times in sexual matters. "If you don't go with history, you don't begin to exist," was what he told me. He had to be appreciated, and I became, somehow, the ideal reflector of his sexual deeds. He was "real life." I was the historian who wrote it up. He said, "Why did you choose Walter Lippmann to do a number on? You should take me instead—representing free sexuality."

"To do a number on?"

"Come on, Harry! As an example. A vanguard figure of the emancipated present age."

It was no secret that I had loved Amy, but that was sophomoric, a high-school crush. No one, of course, had any business to love anybody.

"Why do you suppose I invited you to join us in the shower at the Palmer House?" he said.

The correct answer would have been: to cure me of my sentiments. This was typical of his arrangements—his version of cure or correction in accordance with realistic principles.

I'll say this for my old friend Jay Wustrin: he was stupid about the biggest questions. He approached all the right things for all the wrong reasons, to borrow a turn of phrase from T. S. Elyat, his idol.

Amy, later on that day, when the blizzard crossed the city and fell on the eastern shore of the lake, answered some of my long-unasked questions.

What went on at his New Year's Eve parties had never been hidden from her. "He brought all his lady friends to the house, together with their poor wimp husbands," she said. "It was his big annual production—he loved it. I even accepted phony cocktail dates with those women. I'd meet them in some Near-Northside bar and sit in a booth. Their voices were trembling with guilt and appeasement. Most of them he had by then spun off. . . . He said that he used to tell you about his afternoon parties."

"Some. More or less he kept me posted. I didn't care to hear the blow-by-blow details," I said.

Not true. I looked down on his activities, but I never tired of hearing (translating them into my terms) about these seductions. Of the girls by him. Of him by them. More than forty years of it, starting with women who worked in his father's laundry. On bags of soiled towels and bedding, after five P.M., when his pa put him in charge of locking up for the night.

I remembered his anecdotes when he had long forgotten them.

"I was on an errand for the print shop," he said (one of his side jobs in law school). "In the car at Washington and Michigan, about to turn south, I saw a chick who put her thumb out for a lift. So I opened the door and she got in. She was going to South Shore, and I said I could take her as far as Fifty-seventh Street. But she said, 'What about all the way?' So I took her up on this and said, If you mean all the way, I'll drive you there. You live by yourself? 'Myself.' So I went upstairs with her."

"You could have been mugged and rolled."

"I have an instinct for things like this," he said. "When we undressed, she took my cock in her hand and said, 'Now, here's a *real* cock for you. Let's get it inside, and when it's inside, shoot my heart with it.'"

"Was the woman pretty?"

"Her body was terrifically sexy. She really blitzed me."

What was the good of saying, "She was a nymphomaniac. You get no credit for that." No. With Oriental patience, I held still while he loaded me like a beast of burden with his anecdotes. So that long after he had forgotten, I still remembered his sexual afternoons and evenings. Even his mornings, when, waiting in a doorway, he watched a husband leaving for work.

"Were you giving the woman time to change the bed?"

"Change! Where do you get such an idea! This is the action."

His big eyes, dilated to the limit, demanded your admiration. Heat, crowding, limbs and trunks, lust, dirt, and histrionics. The cameras were always on him. In my generation, these darting on-camera glances were common. Like the movie made of *Street Scene*, by Elmer Rice—the camera moving melodramatically from the crowded East Side street, up the fire escape to the window of the adulteress, while the audience was crazed unaware by suggestive music.

I seemed to Jay to drown my emotions in my face, Chinese style.

Amy had it right. She understood that he briefed me on his sexual activities. Jay believed they were memorable. They should be told.

She asked me more than once whether Jay had played the incriminating tapes for me.

"No," I always said.

"They were heard in chambers. After a few minutes, I asked the judge to excuse me. I admitted that it was my voice, and he said I could go."

"It never occurred to you that Jay had you bugged?"

"Never. And he's always been an obvious man. He couldn't wait to tell you what he was up to. He's not the kind to have long-range cunning silent plans."

"As a divorce lawyer, he must have recommended secret traps to clients, to husbands or to wives."

"Of course. He used to tell me about it. He dealt with several detective agencies," said Amy.

"You didn't think he'd do it to you."

"He lost all interest in me, that way. About ten years ago, we went through the final stages of black

underwear and doing it in front of the mirror. I had
to bend over the back of a chair."

I wished that Amy wouldn't tell me such things.

I told her when I returned from Burma and
Guatemala just how she had figured in my life. Of
course, she didn't know the full extent of it. Nor did
she ask for the particulars. By asking, she would have
opened herself to my questions, and that inevitably
would have brought up the specifics. Better generali-
ties than the minute particulars in such matters.

People like Jay Wustrin present themselves so as
to dramatize or to advertise—they put forth an image.
Their idea of themselves is a public idea. Thus Amy in
her black underwear being done from behind by her
stout husband can become a picture suitable for
framing. Hang it in your guest room. . . . Your inward-
ness should be—deserves to be—a secret about which
nobody needs to get excited. Like the old gag . . .
Q: "What's the difference between ignorance and
indifference?" A: "I don't know, and I don't care."

Nobody much cares about your deepest
secrets. They can matter in politics. John Kennedy's
part in the murder of Diem is worth knowing. His
having women rushed into the Oval Office and
out again makes him no different from other chief
executive officers, situated in Caracas or Macao. I
stress this because with me it has been a lifelong
principle not to disclose anything to those "close" to

me. Moreover, at any deeper level, what is known is just as inexact and fuzzy as the new information you will presently add to the old.

When questioned, I clammed up. Nobody knew what I did in Indochina or Burma. Whether there were women in my life. Or children. Or military dictators. Or Mafia dealings. Or covert intelligence assignments. Or Swiss bank accounts. It may be that I did drown my doings, my nature, in my face. And I never made much of an effort to communicate with Amy. Warmth? Yes. Affection? That too. But after the three of us left the shower stall at the Palmer House and Jay suddenly remembered his court appointment and ran off and I kissed Amy under the breast and inside the thigh, not a word was said about my feelings. Amy's only mention of the threesome in the shower was that Jay had touched me more than he had her.

I said that didn't signify much.

"I was there because of you," I said to her.

"If you cared for me, you could have sent a clearer signal," she said. With her eyes, she led my glance downward to what she had become. She then added, "Nobody seemed able to get through to you. Why were you always so secretive?"

"Well, I was a dishonest kid, and I lied to everybody. I held out on my friends. I cheated, I stole, and I welshed."

"Maybe that was why you had such a non-boyish distinguished look from the first."

"Did I look so special? I had no problem with being dishonest. If I was going to survive, it seemed to me, I had to con everybody."

"Was it because you were a little crook that I fell in love with you?" said Amy. "But then, at the Palmer House, when you had the opportunity, you didn't take it."

I was ready with my answer, having thought and rethought the scene hundreds if not thousands of times. "Just because you were available to me. As you had been available to Jay. . . ."

She said, "It would have been the generic product, as druggists say, not the name brand. Not you and me, but any male with any female. Looking back, I might have felt like a sex tramp."

"Something like. . . ."

"But still it would have been a specific. It would have tied us together."

"I already was tied to you," I said.

This was an uncomfortable exchange, frank on both sides and therefore necessary. From my side, however, it was extremely painful. The reason for this was that I had fallen in love with her when I was an adolescent schoolboy. This tremendous feeling came, as they say, "we know not whence." Everything—but *every*thing!—was as before. There were still kitchens with onions and potato peels in the sink, and streetcars grinding on the rails. So this love, straight and simple, an involuntary music, was an embarrassment to a little crook like me. To the devious secrets (which later made me a "mystery man"), this love, direct, from nature, came over me. I couldn't help being ashamed of the ordinary middle-class character of this connection with Amy. She was a middle-class girl. I was some sort of revolutionist. "You little gonif," my impatient mother used to call me. This didn't signify that I was literally a crook; it meant that I had a masked character. I wasn't about to join the middle class for Amy's sake and be a petty bourgeois. I didn't want to play the hypocrite. It was enough at the time to thicken my mask.

One thing I will say on my own behalf: I wasn't jealous of Jay Wustrin gripping Amy before the wall mirror, or of the New York man whose blow-by-blow sex conversations with her were on the tapes played for the judge in chambers. Causing pain, even committing murder, was justified by the Marquis de Sade as long as it produced intense sexual pleasure. Amy, on tape, wasn't even close—a mere bleep in the worldwide sexual uproar.

I couldn't have expected Amy to mark time while I was inching toward her. It was a lengthy intelligence job for me, cracking one cipher after another. Held up here for a week, there for a decade, I always knew where she was located and what she was up to, more or less.

Of course, she was no longer the beauty she had been. Her face had begun some years earlier to lose its fullness. The sense of her chin today could be completed only if you traced it back to its earlier form. I had no one but myself to blame for what I had missed. Besides, I hadn't absolutely missed it.

It now became clear, like a fuzzy color slide brought suddenly into focus, that I had been in daily contact with Amy, year in, year out, getting support from her in imaginary consultations even about subterranean enterprises or business combinations. Over many years I saw the feelings I had for her as sheer kitsch. And kitsch didn't sort well with the advanced forms of personal development I was after.

Sometimes it seemed to me that Amy had a better than fair understanding of this. With a little luck, you discover that the people in your life, permanently placed, are able to follow your inmost, deeply concealed motives. Now, my dead friend Jay Wustrin had been open, theatrical. I was secretive, uncharitable, prepared to do my neighbor in the eye. Jay *thought* he was open; I *thought* I was closed, and keeping my own counsel.

But Amy was well aware that I turned to her continually and all my efforts to detach myself from her had failed completely. She understood what first love can do. It strikes you at seventeen and, like infantile paralysis, though it works through the heart, not the spinal cord, it, too, can be crippling.

Well, then, was old Adletsky taken in when he recruited me for his brain trust? In his place, would I have recruited him? He had turned from money (the founder of an empire) to personal observation, and he hadn't done badly with Frances Jellicoe and her rowdy drunken husband.

He always spoke of Frances with respect and said that on that occasion I had brought out the observer in him.

"It's not so much a skill, is it, Mr. Trellman. It's a way of life."

"If you have it, it's because you've always had it," I said.

The personal observations Adletsky had made in the course of building his empire were of a different order, inevitably. In an acquisition or a merger, you were partly guided by your banking or cartel specialists, but nevertheless you were sure to come away with your private impressions, your own take, in the cinematic sense, of the participants or principals. I had only a rough idea of what he might have seen in seven or eight decades of such registering and observing. But the emphasis must often have changed. Necessarily, you ran out of stages on life's way—after childhood, manhood, late maturity. For a man of Adletsky's age, then, what could terms like "later" or "earlier" mean? With this in mind, I once told him that Churchill in his final years was maddened by boredom and prayed for death.

Adletsky hadn't been surprised. "In his time, he did everything. Just think what it must have meant for him when there was nothing to do and he had no power left. One day it's Hitler, Roosevelt, *The Hinge of Fate*, then there's nothing at all. Just a lot of worn-out upholstery."

As he spoke, his narrow, beaked face and his thin old venous temples invited me to make what I liked of his words.

He said to me on one of my visits, "I never worry about your writing down or reporting our conversations. You're too reserved and proud of your reserve even to consider it. That is built into you, Harry."

You never dropped in on Mr. Adletsky. You met him only by appointment. But his reason for inviting you was often obscure. He wondered, he recently said, whether I would have a look at Bodo Heisinger's Chinese sideboards and cabinets.

"For that, you'd want somebody from Gump's in San Francisco."

"Well, if the pieces are phonies, I'm sure you could spot them. Couldn't you?"

"Maybe I could."

He filled my brandy glass with his own billionaire's hand. It was like being waited on by Napoleon Bonaparte—Napoleon the prisoner at Saint Helena. There wasn't much for the prisoner to do in exile. Now old age was Adletsky's exile. To fill up his time, the banished Napoleon read hundreds of memoirs, played chess badly, was a poor horseman. He had never liked to ride. There was an abstract grandeur about him, one of his companions in exile said. About Adletsky there was nothing abstract. Now and then something like dreaminess descended on him, but nothing like grandeur. When he asked me to be one of his brain trusters, he had been kidding, of course. For one thing, he would never have claimed the slightest resemblance to Franklin D. Roosevelt. As for Napoleon, Napoleon wouldn't have figured in his thoughts.

On this occasion I felt that there was something heavy or clumsy in my posture. Sitting on a brocaded love seat, I felt lumpish, physically ill-assorted. These interviews often made me uneasy about my supposed powers.

"I think you would be able to spot Bodo's fakes. Though probably Madge bought them," Adletsky continued. Then he veered off into a different subject. "I wonder about you. You set yourself up in Burma and then in Guatemala. You've got it made. Then why do you come back to *this* city? It's a great base for entrepreneurs. But you're not an entrepreneur. So what's here for you? The opera? The Art Institute? Your family? You could be living in New York. Or in Paris."

"Paris is just New York in French."

For a man with so much money, Adletsky had very few gestures. He now turned his hand palm upward, perhaps to say that it never had occurred to him to give ratings to the cities of the world. But in opening his old hand, he might have been inviting me to speak. He was saying, Why not come clean?

That was a possibility too. Well, perhaps I would give it a try. So I simply said to Adletsky, "I have a connection here."

"I see. I see. That's a direct answer. You couldn't get a more direct. This rules out Rangoon, Guatemala City, Paris, New York, and lots of other places. Two on this list, besides, are military dictatorships. And you wouldn't feel easy in a military dictatorship."

"I'm not comfortable in the tropics," I heard myself saying.

I might have added that I was fond of winter, of snow on the ground and the old-fashioned raccoon coats high-school girls used to wear—coats with big braided leather buttons—and that I valued highly the smell of animal musk released from the fur by the warmth of Amy's body when she unfastened those buttons. The heavy round raccoon hat slipped even farther back from her forehead when she pulled me close. Yes, she reached out her arms and pulled me close.

And on the day of the blizzard that passed over Chicago and fell on the eastern edge of Lake Michigan, Adletsky telephoned me in my Van Buren Street hideaway. He said, "Our friend Mrs. Wustrin is going to have a bad day of it at the cemetery. No woman should have to do such a chore alone. Maybe we should lend a hand."

I made some dry answer or other. There was no reason why I should give myself away to him. Adletsky *had* guessed something about my feelings. Maybe he had, after all, learned something from his former brain twister. Confidences, however, would have been out of character. You don't discuss the outlines of your emotional life with one of the richest men in the world—not even if he wants to do you some good. Maybe he saw that my mystery was, at bottom, nothing but misery.

"I'll tell you what I've got in mind," said Adletsky. "Dame Siggy and I will lie down for our siesta soon. I'm sending the limo for you—if you're up to this—with a second driver. Driver number two brings Amy's car back to the garage. Driver number one goes anywhere you say. Are you available today?"

Civil of the old guy to ask. I was very surprised by this. It was as though the chairman of the Federal Reserve were phoning with a question or request. Would I attend the exhumation and reburial of my old friend Wustrin? Would I support Mrs. Wustrin?

She was not strictly speaking his widow. This was something like an institutional intervention in the private sphere.

My answer was minimal. "Okay," I said. "I'll do what I can."

"To add to her trouble budget," said Adletsky, sounding more foreign when he was racy or ingenious (what *was* a "trouble budget"?), "Mrs. Bodo Heisinger poured scalding tea in her lap this morning. She'll surely tell you about it herself." She had gone home to put on dry clothing. She had even applied the aloe vera. It helped. "The one and only useful and true thing I ever heard from Heisinger, that old airhead," Amy said.

From the stretch limo I telephoned the cemetery office. Yes, Mrs. Wustrin had arrived a while back, bringing all the necessary legal papers. She was outside now. Did I need to speak to her?

"No," I said. "My name is Harry Trellman. Just tell her I'm on my way. I'm on a cellular phone." As if it were a novelty. There are tens of millions of cellular phones. *I* didn't own one, though. I am less communicative than most. It was uncharacteristic of me to boast that I was using an advanced instrument.

Of course, I knew the way to the cemetery—I was all too familiar with it. You went due west on the Congress Street Expressway and got off at Harlem Avenue, Chicago's city limit. When I was a boy, there were vacant lots out here. Now there are small industries, taverns, pizza joints, commercial greenhouses, and, of course, the bungalow belt—tens of thousands, hundreds of thousands, of brick bungalows.

I had never made a trip all by myself in this ocean-liner limo. So much soundproofed luxury and kid-leather upholstery, the bar with its cut glass, its brandy decanters.

Composure is one of my special gifts. Not to look impressed. An impervious pre-Columbian look. Maybe it's in the air of this continent. The Red Indians were famous for it, and now the sons and daughters of immigrants can also assume a look of solitary dignity. And there is something about these great limos that makes you think of concert pianos and, in this case, more appropriately, of funerals. In this rolling instrument I passed through the wrought-iron cemetery gates.

Dame Siggy had been right to predict wet ground. There's lots of sandy soil in Chicago. The melting ice of the last glaciation left a huge lake here, and much of the city stands on a series of old beaches. Farther out are the prairies—rolling land such as you must find in central Siberia. So the graves go into the ancient lake bottom, twenty or thirty thousand years old. Big trees don't thrive in this sandy soil. Everything might have been different for us if such trees had grown in the Midwest as they do in the East—smooth-skinned beeches that go back to the eighteenth century. In dense urban ceme-

teries, however, there isn't much room for big trees.
Here you see cottonwoods or catalpas. Gravediggers
have to cut through roots. In the walls of an open
grave you always see the white butts of severed roots.

The chauffeur was piloted by a guide waiting
for him inside the gate. For the rich, such arrangements are laid on beforehand. This was not a large
cemetery. In it, the relatively small Jewish neighborhoods of Chicago were represented, so that even I,
whose contact with the Jewish community was minimal, could recognize many of the names.

Amy had followed Mrs. Adletsky's advice and
put on boots. I saw her as soon as I lowered the sepia-
tinted window. Her back was to the road. The diggers were already at work, and there was a little
winch coming up—a rig something like a backhoe, I
thought, with the driver on a high seat. A van was
waiting to carry Jay's coffin to its permanent grave.
He would be reburied between his parents.

Blizzard, thaw, brief sunlight, and then gloom
again. A cloud as tall as England had just crossed the
sun. Under bare branches and through the daggers of
pruned bushes, the soil was piling up. Amy didn't
recognize the limousine that had come for her that
very morning; nor was she expecting me to come out
when the chauffeur opened the door. In my low but
coherent voice (a lifelong training in articulate but
deferential speech: I myself would be reluctant to

trust a man who spoke as I did), I explained what Sigmund Adletsky had arranged. "It was his idea," I said. Her look was silent and reserved, even a little bleak. Looking beyond me, she glanced here and there, trying to put it all together. Considering the circumstances, I couldn't blame her. She was unable to guess how much I had told Adletsky about her. And I could readily picture what she was seeing—my hair still thick, straight and black, and my narrow forehead, incurved like a low bluff, then black Chink eyes, on the small side, in what is probably the densest part of my face. And, finally, my mother's thick mouth—even thicker than hers. My hands were in my coat pockets, thumbs on the outside.

"This driver is here to take your car back," I said. "I'll keep you company in the limo. . . ."

"It's kind of Mr. Adletsky," she said.

I was about to say that at ninety-two, Adletsky was pioneering in compassion, a new field for him. But I held back.

"Let's tell the driver to park this glamorous machine. Then we can sit down, get out of the cold air. It's still got a wicked sting, even late in March. If I lower the window a bit, we can keep an eye on things."

So she and I sat in the luxurious swivel chairs—silent at first, but presently quite a conversation developed.

"What's with your old father?" I said.

"Alzheimer's disease has pretty well swallowed up his mind. These last years, he does recognize me on and off."

It followed that he was expected to die soon. If she had had to store or bury him temporarily, while Jay was moved, the complications would have been unpleasant.

"My mother expected to have Dad lie alongside."

"She didn't care for Jay, did she?"

"She said the Wustrins were common and Jay made crude jokes. He was almost too much for her to bear."

"Well, it was his idea of a joke to buy the grave from your dad—like getting into a double bed with his mother-in-law. Poor Jay was obviously dying. If it was clear to you and me, it was even more clear to him. I'd meet him around town and he'd smile, but he didn't force his company on me. He became self-effacing. He went from a fat man to a thin boy. And when he gave up his office, his practice, he gave up on neatness."

"As long as he was chasing, he still groomed himself," said Amy. "But all that time, he was planning to make trouble for me."

"So that he shouldn't be forgotten. You were going to live on, and he didn't see why he shouldn't arrange a little trouble for you."

"You're smiling about it."

"Who can say what curious things people are thinking when they consider what death will be like? I mean, how their death will affect the living. 'What will the world be without me?'"

"A childish idea."

"He didn't like being alone. When we were kids, he used to force me to go into the toilet with him. You weren't going to get rid of him so easily."

"So now we're spending an afternoon in the cemetery with him," said Amy.

"This is a better place than most for assessments, if you're going to assess."

Amy had thrown back her coat at the shoulders; it was warm inside the great black limo—the engine was idling. So that when she shrugged, the soft breasts in her sweater added weight to her shrug. "What's to assess? Why would you want to pick on yourself, even here? You have obscure ways and habits, Harry. Years ago, when I had to think seriously about you, I took your quirks into consideration. Given the kinks of your high-level mental life, there was not a chance that you could ever think well of me. And I did give you serious thought. I was in love with you. But nobody else's views were ever good enough for you. You'd put them down. And I thought: Maybe he loves me, but I'll never know what he's thinking. In his mind,

he puts me down too. . . . Your classification for me
was 'a petty-bourgeois broad.' "

"You never told me that before," I said, and
then I didn't know how to continue. We had gotten
along for decades without each other. Separate
arrangements were made. All the while, I had con-
cluded that I was too odd for her. Or that for various
other reasons she assumed I could never be domesti-
cated. So my emotions went into storage, more or
less permanently. But by and by I began to see what
sort of hold she had on me. Other women were
apparitions. She, and only she, was no apparition.

"Yes, but I had more feeling for you than you
realize. What I felt was very simple. You gave me relief
from double-entry mental bookkeeping," I said. "I used
to think if there was a bare room in your house, without
anything in it, not even a carpet, it would do me good
to go in and lie face down on the wooden floor. . . ."

The gravediggers, whom we saw from time to
time by bending double, glancing through the open
bar of light, seemed to be taking their time. Such
work I was no longer fit for. Digging kept them fit.
No NordicTrack necessary. This digging was labor of
the ancient sort, when prisoners worked the treadmill
and slaves went to the fields with picks and spades.

Amy appeared to be thinking of what I had said.
We had very seldom been together like this. From time
to time we'd meet for cocktails or dinner, and generally

we talked about the Merchandise Mart, the decorating business, Burmese furniture, and copperwork. I became useful to Amy. I had vouched for her to the Adletskys, and they had recommended her to other rich clients. She was grateful to me. Her business prospects were our principal topic at the Szechuan Restaurant or Coco Pazzo or Les Nomades. Two dilatory people who had loved each other for forty years, discussing ottomans and wing chairs. I had never said anything about stretching out on her wooden floor.

And now, too, but for the fact that Jay's coffin was being exhumed, we might have been chatting in a luxurious little parlor with the TV screens shining cokey gray, iridescent, and a small bar and cellular telephones.

"Did Madge Heisinger really pour tea in your lap? Were you scalded?"

"No, no. I was shocked but not actually burned. That's just how she does things. She wanted to talk privately. She had a proposition for me, and she thought we should get together in the bathroom, where nobody could disturb us."

The proposition Amy heard was this—the money the Adletskys paid for the furniture in the apartment was to go to Madge. Bodo agreed that she should have it and with this money she would start up business. She would open a divorce registry service. The opposite to a bridal registry. When a marriage breaks up, one of the divorcing parties generally takes all. The deprived husband or the stripped wife needs outfitting in all the essentials of housekeeping—a bed, two chairs, a carpet, a blanket, linens, coffeemaker, skillet, tooth glass, cups, spoons, towels, down to the clock radio or TV. Since recently divorced company employees are often agitated, suffering weeks or months of stress, they function badly, and personnel directors in the giant corporations might welcome such a registry service. It wouldn't cost the company money, because your fellow employees or business associates would contribute to a divorce fund to ease the shocks of dislocation, rejection, the pains of loss. It would on one side be excellent for the morale and on the other profitable for the suppliers of the survival kit. Amy, with her Merchandise Mart contacts, could easily, dependably—uniformly—procure such items. This would give divorcées parity with brides. It would stress equality. It would have a democratic flavor. For a small showroom, the overhead would be minimal.

I laughed when I heard this. "Yes, I've got the picture," I said. "Now, who would deal with the corporate personnel officers? Who'd do the persuading?"

"According to Madge, that would be Tom's part of it," Amy said.

"Tom is the fellow who was supposed to blow Bodo away—is that right?"

"Yes. Madge feels responsible. She got him into it. There were three years in the slammer, plus months of pretrial, trial, and appeal. Madge says she should take the blame. She insists that it's her responsibility, that she *owes* him."

"You never laid eyes on this Tom?"

"How should I? I don't mix with people that hang out in bars. Cruising and picking up men in joints is not my kind of thing. I understand it happens a lot in ticket lines at the movies. You can judge the person standing in the queue by the kind of film it is. Or at the Art Institute, where guys on the make hang out—studs who pretend to love painting."

She sharply resented any hint that she in any way resembled the woman whose screams were recorded by Jay's divorce detectives and auditioned in chambers. The judge stuck in her throat. Judges without exception were on the take, she said, and you couldn't build a prison big enough to hold all the Chicago judges who were eligible.

"I wonder, since Madge was setting up a business relationship, whether she suggested a meeting. What's this Tom supposed to be like?"

"You may have seen him on TV during the trial. . . . As a business idea it's not unimaginative," said Amy.

I kept laughing at the absurdity of the whole plan. "Mrs. Heisinger gets intricate ideas," I said. "If this is the way the murder was planned, no wonder Bodo took the gun away from Tom. Madge belongs to the Jay Wustrin school of real-life fantasy."

"You mean mapping out such elaborate brainstorm scenarios. He did love them, didn't he. So tell me, Harry, what do you make of it all?"

The diggers would soon be waist deep. If Adletsky had not sent me here today, Amy would have been walking among the tombstones alone, studying the names, doing cemetery arithmetic. Subtract 1912 from 1987. The air, though faintly sunny, had a sharp edge.

Under all the influence of the day and the place, I took new readings on Amy, revising the life-long familiar ones. For instance, her eyes were as round as always, but there was now a childish sobriety about them. Odd, this child look appearing in middle age, especially since her cheeks were no longer perfectly smooth and much of her color was lost. But she was essentially still Amy. If you turned the little chiming crank and said, "Hello, Central," Amy at Central would answer.

She was waiting for my comments. When I moved, I saw my silhouette in the gray bosom of the limo TV—the black lank hair and the familiar desperately unwanted Chinese profile. Reflected on the screen, I was bulky. I was somewhere between a shadow and a shade of one of the departed. Having for years been a deliberate mystery to others, I find that I am unable now to say what the mystery was about or why mystification ever was necessary.

A considerable amount of soil had come out—dark-brown earth mixed with human qualities.

"Here's what I think . . . ," I said.

"Speak clearly. I need smart, definite advice."

"Okay, I'll start by saying that I love to give advice. I only recently realized that I used to be reserved about it. But I love advising. A nice bit of advice can bring tears to my eyes. I'll try not to mumble. People do who talk to themselves a lot."

"When I found out that Adletsky chose you for his brain trust, I realized that I had overlooked something," said Amy.

"Yes? I rose in your esteem? And yet we've known each other for a lifetime, almost."

"Old Adletsky must believe you can help me—that you want to do it."

"And that I'd be ideal company for an exhumation."

"I really can't take that word. It came up again and again when I applied for the papers. Let's say a reburial. . . . I don't suppose anybody knew Jay longer than you."

"Are you considering Madge's proposition?"

"Do you think the old guy figured Madge poured tea on me because she wanted us to be alone for a private moment?"

"He's very quick to make connections. Anyway, he intuits my feeling for you. He's picked up quite a few subliminal hints. . . ."

"Please, Harry—louder. Most of your communication has got to be inward, so that even when you're with somebody else you more than half talk to yourself."

I think very fast, then I edit the thoughts just as quickly. But it's hard for speech to keep up. It may be the thick lips that make articulation difficult.

"To finish with Adletsky. I have a most basic lifelong feeling toward you, Amy. It's something not possible to conceal from a skillful observer. In my feelings, I've always had an open direct line to you. It's from my nature, not from my character. My character is compromised. But not even a compromised—okay, a mutilated character could change my nature."

"I don't exactly follow that, but has old Mr. Adletsky been able to pick up something so deeply buried?"

I said, "You must be aware that dealing with someone like Madge Heisinger, you have to prepare for all kinds of perversity. You can't count on the business side of the relationship—the proposed relationship. You must consider the proposition separately."

"Separate it from what?"

"Why, is she a businesswoman? Or is she a psychopath, a crazy, a sociopath, a criminal?"

"I understand you one hundred percent," said Amy. "In your mind, just for the interest of it, what does this come to?"

"I see the logic she's following," I said.

"I fail to see any."

"We have to see her idea as she sees it: because and because and because. Now, therefore . . . when you're in jail, among women who describe their lives to one another, something like a motive may develop to get some good, to extract it from so much bad, and in our country something good is most usually a business idea—the imagination of a profitable enterprise. In other words, 'How would it be if . . . ?' 'Or, here's a million-dollar idea!' So your aberrations lead to a conclusion that recruits you to your country and returns you to your civilization."

I can't swear that Amy was following this. Over a long time, she had probably taught herself to write off sixty percent of what I said. As a friend of the family, I did often sound off at the Wustrins' dinner table.

"She was going to persuade Bodo to get her out of jail. There'd be a new deal for them both," I said. "Bodo would be able to proclaim how decent it was of him to let her out—how big of him. Also how brave it was to take her back. Also, it was a boost for love. He was a stand-up guy with love in his heart. He was confident of his manhood and showed it by remarrying Madge. It was extremely newsworthy too—millions of dollars' worth of free publicity. And he's no chump. Except that he thinks he's a bigger man than anybody could ever have guessed."

"But Madge's divorce registry?" Amy reminded me.

"How many prisoners in the women's wing had been married more than once?"

"Was there some woman in prison who thought up the business? Isn't it also possible that Madge's guy, Tom, came up with the idea that divorcing couples, like brides and grooms, should register for gifts? And that they could make a business of it?"

"It is possible, isn't it," I said. "That also would explain why he has to be included."

"And she thinks she can trust me with the boyfriend. I'm too old for him," said Amy.

"Several possibilities follow. It could be a smart business. I mean fashionable. It'll attract notice because it's ingenious, because it has a comic wrinkle based on the bridal registry custom. The newspapers will pick it up. So will TV. If friends can give wedding presents, they can also come forward when a marriage goes sour."

"Could you suggest how Madge fits me into this?"

"I think I might . . . ," I said, being tentative.

"Then go ahead."

"She figured in a murder plot. You were part of a notorious divorce. You were cleaned out by Jay—"

"Of course I was. I didn't have so much as a coffee cup left. Add me to those two from the prison, and we would make a real freak trio in a tiny show-room at the Merchandise Mart, with desks, bright lights, and telephones. It made me laugh when Madge described it. She spoke of TV programs. Maybe Oprah Winfrey. She's so absolutely high-handed and crazy that I thought just for that reason it might make money."

"Junior corporate employees might get a kick out of it. It suggests an advanced countercultural lifestyle."

"You're perfectly right, Harry."

"And you'd be invaluable to Madge. You'd attract the columnists and reporters. The talk shows certainly would be dying to book you. *Vanity Fair* and magazines like *Hustler* would pursue you."

"I couldn't bear it," said Amy.

"Well, in the eighteenth century, some serious person or other wrote about 'wanton and disorderly mirth,' also 'the vices of levity.' It may have been Adam Smith. I'd be surprised if Madge wasn't on the same track."

Round-eyed, Amy stared at me and then stared past me. Presently she said, "I couldn't possibly . . . Naturally, I'd be the third member of a scandal team. Madge would make me just that. I saw the truth of it as soon as you said it."

"You'd have found out yourself, in short order."

"Yes, but maybe not in time."

"Well, I'm glad I was able to put this glamorous proposition in perspective. One comment, if you'll allow me to make it, is that goods are always available—all the kitchenware, clock radios, bed linens, TV sets, coffeemakers. . . . Commodities all the way to the horizon. There's enough of everything for everybody. That's how productive and rich the social order is. The whole process began with the proposition that the conquest of nature was going to be the top job of the modern age. . . ."

Listening, Amy gradually lowered her head, as if to be particularly attentive—or perhaps to let me have my way, to wait me out. I had always said such things. When we were younger, Amy used to say, "Here we go again." I think she disliked—at times positively hated—such remarks about the social order or the modern age. They reduced her to a lower mental rank. When I aired my deeper views, she waited me out. She made allowance for this minor vice. These observations seemed worth making, and against my better judgment I made them. Occasionally I couldn't resist trying them out at the dinner table.

"Jay picked up this habit from you, Harry," she had once complained. "In our Northside days, when we were first married. And especially when he was playing Bartók LPs, he'd get his ass up against the chimneypiece and put his elbows on the mantel and start quoting his T. S. Eliot to me. And as you know, I'm not one of those women who are born to be deep. There never has been anything metaphysical about me. I have a high-average IQ, that's all."

But now the diggers were signaling to the fellow who operated the hoist, and his rig approached closer to the edge of the grave.

"I think they're about to begin," I said.

"I was expecting it to take a lot more time."

"Jay hasn't been here long. Not in cemetery terms. The soil hasn't had time to harden."

The tractor tires were printing their treads in the fresh brown dirt. A sort of bay leaf pattern. The smooth little machine stopped in a heap of dark-brown grave soil, and the driver came down and chocked the wheels. Canvas bands were clipped to the coffin, and the hoist was attached. The man who bent to do this was unusually long in the spine. He proved to be short-legged as well. When he stepped back and straightened himself, he wasn't all that tall. The engine started, and the blue-gray coffin tilted from the gravel. The workers straightened it as it rose, dribbling dirt. Unwanted pictures of what was inside went through my head: the body dressed in its business suit, the handsome symmetrical face— cyanotic, chlorotic, livid. Perhaps a forgotten pencil in a pocket. Maybe the shoes were laced, even knotted. Perhaps the dead man had an erection.

The chauffeur came to the door of the limo to help Amy out. I stood at her back, my fingers interknit behind me.

It was Jay Wustrin's theatrical will to come back from the grave. That was why the deal was made with Amy's father. As kids fifty-odd years ago, he and I had seen so many grave movies with Boris Karloff or Bela Lugosi. Lonely churchyards in the Carpathians, gloomy castles in the background. When the Count of Monte Cristo escaped from the Château d'If, Jay, who was wildly excited, said that I was cold-blooded. My answer was: "I'm not going to let them lay all kinds of feelings on me."

"*I'm* the one with the heart!" Jay declared. "You're too remote a one."

In the stretch limo, a world unto itself, as much so in the cemetery as on Michigan Boulevard, we slowly followed the van. "This is all Jay's idea. *He* got us out here, this winter day," said Amy. "Even though in the last year or two he was so thin, so meek. He was looking for familiar faces, and people were cutting him, which normally would have driven him wild—"

"I admit I avoided him too."

"Why did you?"

"A business matter. Money from Burma he was supposed to be holding for me. *I* wasn't supposed to have any such money, and I sent it by messenger. He signed receipts when he took it. Then, when I asked for it, he said he'd have to pay it back in installments."

"It's the first I hear of this."

"No reason why you should have heard. And actually Jay was a generous friend. He never forgot my birthday. He made me fine gifts—a beautiful set of Jowett's Plato, and *The Decline and Fall* in an old edition. I still own them, read them. I occasionally try to tell people what's in them."

"Tell me about the Burma money. . . ."

"That was hanky-panky. Let's not go into it."

"It's your call," said Amy. "But his body had to be moved. I couldn't have my parents separated. My mother would never forgive it. What if my dad did lose his marbles? After fifty years of the marriage bed, her wish was that it should be eternal."

Just as Amy and Jay had for decades slept nude together, inhaling each other's odors, her hands familiar with the man's body hair. Even her face creams and his night grunts would have entered into it. And shared cakes of soap and clothes closets and dinners—such a complex of intimacies.

One can give such particulars too much value. Bourgeois habits have no claim to be sanctified or eternalized. All that is mainstream stuff, and I've never really been a mainstream type. I've always been a fairly hard judge of people. Especially if they thought too well of themselves—were proud of their intelligence or believed they knew everything there was to know about the British Empire or the U.S. Constitution—I put them down, no quarter given, no margin for mercy. So why should I go easy on Jay Wustrin! He married the only woman I had ever loved, and he made an utter fuck-up of their life together.

So then . . .

We are, for the time being, the living, maimed and defective. And, today, in strange circumstances—riding in a multibillionaire's stretch limo, the kind with amber windows and a TV aerial boomerang mounted on the trunk. And following the remains of an old pal who, for an interval (two hours), arranged to escape from the grave.

Any one of the headstones we passed but couldn't see through the immunizing, smoked limo windows might have been that of my father (my mother was buried in Arizona). You wouldn't expect such a personality as mine to go for family piety. I hadn't been out in the cemetery for years and years.

Hereabouts our neighbors and some of our schoolmates lay buried.

If I'm going to do anything at all before my turn comes, I thought, I'd better begin to make my moves.

"Has it all been arranged? For Jay, I mean. If we should arrive with his coffin and no grave waiting . . ."

"Oh, it's dug. I took care of that.... What really worried me was that the casket might open when it was being lifted. I thought the body might fall out."

"It crossed my mind too," I said. "But it couldn't happen. These guys know their job. It's routine, and the equipment is complete. They lay the coffin on those canvas bands, and then the little engine starts up, and in one smooth minute the coffin is lying on the bottom.... You have the look of thinking something special, Amy."

"Something like musical chairs, as they used to be played in kindergarten," she said. "When the piano stopped, you dropped into an empty seat. Getting buried in my dad's grave was Jay's idea of a witty thing."

And how did *I* fit into this picture? My seldom barbered, spiky black hair, chub lips. Yes, and those concave shins you saw again and again, leafing through Hokusai. I kept a fat book of his drawings in my office on Van Buren Street. Yet Amy and I, as high-school sophomores, had often had petting parties, as they used to be called. She had liked me well enough then. We kissed madly and gripped each other. I sank my face in the musky damp of the raccoon fur.

"There's something I have to ask you, Harry," said Amy. "I've been fighting it, but I can't help asking one more time. I've never had a satisfactory answer. Did you or did you not listen to me on tape?"

I held my breath for a few pulses; then, like the practiced liar that I am, I denied it again. But sometimes the truth will hitch a short ride with your finest lies. I saw that she didn't believe me, so I passed to what was more important. I said, "Listening wouldn't have changed a whole lifetime of feeling. First you married Berner and had kids by him. We were in the shower together."

"Yes."

"Jay had a wife then. You were still married to Berner. Only a year earlier, I had eloped with Mary. Next thing I knew, you were Jay's wife. My feeling for you remained what it was."

"Though there were other men too, you mean," Amy said.

No. Only the man in New York who had made her scream so on the tape. Of other men, nothing was recorded.

"Well, the young woman in the shower was already an experienced young woman." I didn't want to discuss it. My aim was to get all this behind us.

"There wouldn't be any way to deny it. . . . But you loved me."

"After forty years of thinking it over, the best description I could come up with was 'an actual affinity.' "

"You never did have any use for the way other people spoke, or speak. Everything has to be translated into your own language. But what made it actual?"

"Other women might remind me of you, but there was only one actual Amy."

"But what you heard on the tape that convicted me was my actual voice. Your affinity was screaming."

I made a special effort to speak smoothly, saying, "Well, we all understand what our condition is. It's an age of liberation. It's like a great ship, and the passengers are always trampling toward the port side, or stampeding to starboard, and about to capsize. Never evenly distributed. Just now we're concentrated on the left, the port side. Jay was a leader in the liberation rush. Therefore he should have expected you to retaliate."

"Is that what they mean when they talk about the sexual revolution? But where does that leave you with your actual affinity?"

"I can't say where it leaves me, but it's all I really care about."

Her thoughts turned again to the grave bought half a century ago and held open, reserved for Jay. He would lie beside his father. "I wonder exactly why his mother was such an embarrassment to him."

I said, "He convinced himself that his limitations were inherited from her. He always said, 'You should be able to divorce mothers too.' His dad was a witty, kidding old guy. Old Wustrin had a jumping mind. But he was dead at sixty. She was the tenacious one and died at eighty. She was an obstacle to Jay. She gave away his game."

You could picture Jay Wustrin, as he lay in his coffin in the van ahead, confirming this opinion. To be talked about would have made him so happy. By having himself buried beside his mother-in-law, he was doing a tease. It made you wonder whether he really understood what death was, since in death he tried to make himself still felt. Speaking for myself, my opinion was that eternity would trash all human impulses. Eternity would make you sick of existing.

"I feel uncomfortable in this stretch limo," said Amy. "Riding in it is too much like a funeral procession. It was the same this morning, on the way to the Heisingers'."

"We can get rid of it and go home in a taxi."

Of course, the gravel road with its potholes was nothing to this overriding monster of smoothness that carried us forward. You didn't even hear the tires. I wished that somehow my composure were as good as the shock absorbers and the computerized engine. All the usual resources had left me, and I sat exposed, with my spiky black hair, large cheeks, and speechless chub lips. I had trained myself to give nothing away. At this moment I was vulnerably visible. But Amy wasn't looking at me.

"I don't feel guilty toward Jay," she said. "Somehow I don't."

"I believe he played the tapes to everybody he could get hold of, to show that he was too big a man to be hurt. But he was hurt just the same."

"We're stopping," said Amy.

Now that we had come to the place, her need to get out was urgent. She didn't wait for the chauffeur. She threw open the door and strode over the pale March turf. Her cloth ulster was fully buttoned. I wondered whether she would wear a raccoon coat if I were to buy one for her.

I followed her to the new grave. It was neatly prepared. Here were the canvas bands again, ready for the coffin. I looked at the oval photos set into the headstones. Old Wustrin wore the clipped mustache that I remembered, and an old-fashioned high collar. He held his head at an intelligent angle. Jay's mother was photographed in a silk dress, with bangs cut straight on her welcoming face. Come one, come all. But she was indifferent to everyone. She still cared for nobody but her son.

I offered Amy my pocket handkerchief. She didn't dry her tears but covered her mouth with it.

The back of the van opened, and the coffin was eased forward. To my surprise, the chauffeur volunteered as a pallbearer. There were no prayers said; no ceremony had been arranged. The coffin was set in place. A button was pressed, and the swift, smooth, soundless little engine went into action. When the coffin reached bottom, the gravediggers slipped the bands from beneath and picked up the spades they had stuck in the soil.

I stood back from myself and looked into Amy's face. No one else on all this earth had such features. This *was* the most amazing thing in the life of the world.

The coffin was waiting to be covered. And the backhoe chattered and then roared and made an abrupt run at the soil, printing more laurel-leaf tracks behind. Taking Amy by the hand, I said, "It's not the best moment for a marriage offer. But if it's a mistake, it won't be my first one with you. This is the time to do what I'm now doing, and I hope you'll have me."